THE F...

"Is *that* Peer...

cousin, Marci...

"Isn't he gorgeous...

back.

It was all Jennifer could do to nod in reply. Peer Finstad was the best looking boy, if you could call him a boy, she'd ever seen. He was at least six feet tall and quite muscular. His hair was jet black and he was wearing dark glasses. Peer had on faded jeans, a faded flannel shirt, and well-worn leather boots. As he came toward them Jennifer noticed that he had an easy way of walking, loose and confident. She decided he could easily have been a movie star instead of a fishing guide.

"You give the girls a hand up to their cabin, Peer," Mr. Finstad instructed.

"Okay, Dad," Peer said. He slowly took off his dark glasses. His eyes were deep, deep brown but sparkled with mischief. Then he slipped his sunglasses into his shirt pocket, and somehow managed to pick up both of Marcia's suitcases and Jennifer's bag as well. "Come on," he said with a smile. "Your cabin is right this way."

BANTAM SWEET DREAMS ROMANCES

The Perfect Catch

Laurie Lykken

BANTAM BOOKS
TORONTO • NEW YORK • LONDON • SYDNEY • AUCKLAND

RL 6, IL age 11 and up

THE PERFECT CATCH

A Bantam Book/February 1990

*Bantam Books are published by Bantam Books, a division of Bantam
Doubleday Dell Publishing Group, Inc. Its trademark, consisting of
the words "Bantam Books" and the portrayal of a rooster, is Regis-
tered in U.S. Patent and Trademark Office and in other countries.
Marca Registrada. Bantam Books, 666 Fifth Avenue, New York,
New York 10103.*

Printed and bound in Great Britain by
Cox & Wyman Ltd., Reading

The Perfect Catch

Chapter One

"Finished at last!" Jennifer Garrett said. She felt relieved as she took the last pair of clean jeans out of the clothes basket and folded them into a neat rectangle. "Now all I need is a suitcase." Setting the jeans on her bed with her other clean clothes, Jennifer started toward her bedroom door.

"Where are you going?" Jennifer's best friend, Kate McClusky, asked lazily. Kate was stretched out on Jennifer's guest bed. Kate had slept there so often that the bed seemed to belong to her.

Turning back to face her friend, Jennifer said, "I'm going to the attic to find a suitcase. Want to come?"

"Of course," Kate said, springing to her feet,

1

blond curls bouncing. "I love your attic. Let's go rummage in it!"

"There'll be no rummaging today, McClusky," said Jennifer in a mock-serious tone. "I have too much packing left to do."

Kate threw her arm across Jennifer's shoulders as the girls started down the Garrett's upstairs hall. "You pack, and I'll rummage," she said. "Deal?"

"Deal." Jennifer laughed, wondering how she was going to get along for an entire month without Kate.

"You're excited about your trip, aren't you?" Kate asked.

"Sure—wouldn't you be? I think the last time I went on a trip was three years ago when we drove to the capitol." Jennifer stopped walking and stretched her arms above her head. "Look out world, here comes Jennifer Garrett!"

"I can see why you're so psyched," Kate said. "A whole month on a private island. But don't you hate leaving Mark at the pool all month without someone to guard him?"

"No," Jennifer answered honestly. "Mark and I said goodbye yesterday. He's glad I'm getting a chance to travel, and I'm glad he's getting a chance to be a lifeguard." Jennifer smiled, remembering the tender farewell she'd shared with her boyfriend. "Everything's fine there. We care about each other, but we're way too young to tie ourselves down. I really hope he goes out with other girls while I'm gone. I know I'll go out with other guys if I have the chance."

"The scary thing is, I think you really mean it," Kate said. "Only *you* would be glad if your boyfriend dated someone else."

Jennifer laughed. "You make it sound like I'm nuts."

Kate nodded. "That's because you are."

Jennifer stopped at the top of the attic steps to turn on the light. Instantly, much of the junk her parents had accumulated over seventeen years of married life became visible.

"Oh!" Kate cried, "just look at all this stuff!"

"No," Jennifer told her firmly. "We're only looking for one thing up here. A suitcase. My aunt, uncle and cousin will be here any minute."

"Wow! Look at this box of pictures," Kate exclaimed, ignoring Jennifer's instructions. She collapsed next to the big red box and immediately began digging through it.

"You can look. I don't have time," Jennifer insisted, but she couldn't help stealing a glance at the box herself. She hadn't looked through those pictures in ages.

"It'll only take a minute. I just want to see if I can find a picture of your cousin in here."

"Why?" Jennifer asked. "She's going to be here in the flesh any moment now. Why bother looking for a picture of her?"

"Because I'm curious," Kate said, pulling out picture after picture.

"Oh, all right," Jennifer said, sitting down next to Kate. "I guess a few minutes won't hurt. I'm almost ready to go anyway."

"Now you sound more like the Jen I know," Kate said, pausing in her search to grin at her best friend. Jennifer playfully punched Kate lightly on the arm and tried to grab the box out of her friend's hands.

"Here's a great picture of you!" Kate cried suddenly. "You look like a little princess with your hair in French braids like this, Jen. And what a great dress! It must be all hand-embroidered lace! Do you still have it? When was this picture taken anyway?" Kate asked.

"I don't remember having a dress like that. . . ." Jennifer took the picture from Kate, curious.

"Hey, this isn't a picture of me!" Jennifer exclaimed. "It's a picture of my cousin Marcia. I bet she was about six years old when this was taken."

"Oh wow! You two could be twins!" Kate declared, taking the picture back and examining it more closely.

Jennifer shrugged. "We've both got dark hair and blue eyes, I guess. Say, isn't that a suitcase over there?" she asked, getting to her feet.

"It's more than just your hair and eyes," Kate said, her eyes still examining the face in the picture. "You *really* look alike! You've got the same mouth, straight nose and nice cheekbones. You've even got the same dimple in your right cheek when you smile."

"That was taken years ago," Jennifer said as she retrieved the suitcase. It was kind of beat up, but it would do. "We may have looked alike as kids, but I bet we're really different now."

"Well, I guess we'll see soon enough, won't we?" Kate said.

"I guess we will." Jennifer glanced down at the picture Kate was still holding. "I've only seen Marcia a couple of times before, and the last time was several years ago. I wonder what she's like now."

"I bet she still has beautiful clothes," Kate ventured. "Didn't you say her family was rich?"

Jennifer nodded and headed toward the attic stairs with the suitcase. "I've got what I came for. We'd better hurry."

"Can I bring this picture down?" Kate asked.

Jennifer smiled. "Sure. Why not?" Then, faintly, they heard the doorbell ring.

"It's them!" Kate cried, leaping up excitedly. Then she bolted down the attic stairs.

"Slow down, Kate!" Jennifer said, hurrying after her. "Wait for me!"

Jennifer caught up with Kate at the top of the hall stairs just as Jennifer's mother was opening the front door.

5

"Ben!" Mrs. Garret cried as Jennifer's burly uncle came through the front door first. Ben Brewster had the same blue eyes as Jennifer's mother, the eyes Jennifer's father referred to as "Brewster eyes." Jennifer had them, too, as did her cousin Marcia.

Jennifer was examining her uncle, whom she hadn't seen in quite a few years, when Marcia strolled in. She was dressed in a beige silk suit, her long dark hair drawn together at the nape of her neck with a large, rust-colored bow that matched her rust-colored blouse. Jennifer felt a little uncomfortable in her favorite faded blue jeans, oversized red and white striped rugby shirt, and bare feet. Next to her cousin, she knew she looked like a mess. She had an urge to turn around and run back to her room to change, but it was too late for that now. Remembering the picture Kate had found, Jennifer suspected Marcia would outdress her no matter what she wore.

"Jennifer!" cried Uncle Ben enthusiastically, giving her a big hug as she reached the bottom of the stairs. "I'd know you anywhere. You've got that Brewster look about you! And who's this with you?"

"Uncle Ben, Marcia, I'd like you to meet my best friend, Kate McClusky. Kate lives next door," Jennifer replied once her uncle had released her.

"Hi," Kate said, smiling and wiggling her fingers in a salute.

"Where's Mona?" Mrs. Garrett asked, tilting her head to look around her brother at the still open front door.

"My wife decided to stay in Europe," Uncle Ben replied. Reaching behind him, Uncle Ben pushed the door shut.

"Oh, no!" Jennifer's mother cried. "How will you and the girls be able to manage without her?"

Uncle Ben smiled. "Mona and I go our separate ways quite a bit. Both Marcia and I are used to it. Aren't we, honey?" Marcia looked briefly at her father, then looked away without a word. "Besides," Uncle Ben continued after a moment, "we've got the Finstads to look after us."

"Aren't they that young couple you hired as caretakers when you first bought the island for your business?" Mrs. Garrett asked.

Ben laughed. "They aren't so young anymore, Betsy. The Finstads have three grown sons. Two of them have even left home already. They've just got Peer, their youngest, with them now. Anyway, we'll do just fine." He put his arm around Marcia and gave her shoulder a squeeze. "Right, honey?"

"Right," Marcia said, after pausing a few dramatic seconds, but she didn't sound convincing.

7

Jennifer's mother smiled at Marcia and said, "We haven't seen you in a long time, Marcia. You've turned into a beautiful young woman."

"Thank you," Marcia said, sounding very stiff.

"So, you're Marcia!" Kate said, enthusiastically. "You know, you and Jennifer could almost be twins."

Marcia fixed her steely, blue eyes on Kate. But before she was able to comment on Kate's remark, Jennifer's mother said, "Why don't you girls go on up to Jennifer's room now and get re-acquainted? I'll call you when dinner is ready. You will stay for dinner, won't you, Kate?"

Kate looked quickly at Jennifer and wrinkled her nose. Grinning, she said, "Sure, thanks. That would be nice." Then, turning toward Marcia, Kate said, "Here, Marcia. I'll help you with your stuff." Marcia handed Kate one of her suitcases, and followed Jennifer upstairs.

"So, this is your room," Marcia said, stopping in the doorway. "Cute."

"Well, it's a mess right now, of course," Jennifer said defensively. She imagined seeing her bulletin board covered with pictures of horses and her favorite rock stars, the orange and black pompoms hanging over her bed, even the clutter on her desk and dresser through Marcia's eyes. It all seemed so childish suddenly. "I've been packing."

"Of course," Marcia said, stepping gingerly over the pile of shoes in the doorway.

"We just found this picture of you," Kate said, taking the picture out of her pocket and handing it to Marcia. "We were just admiring the lace dress you're wearing in it. Do you still have it?"

Marcia sat down carefully on a chair, then put the picture down on Jennifer's desk. "I doubt it," she said after a minute. "We don't really have just one place we call home, you know, like this." She made a gesture encompassing all of the Garrett's house. "It's hard to accumulate much stuff when you're always on the move," she said. "Anyway, mother has a million charities she's always donating things to. She probably boxed it up and sent it off the day after this picture was taken."

"Oh," Kate said. For once, Jennifer noted, even Kate seemed to be at a loss for words.

"Well, I suppose I should finish packing," Jennifer said after an uncomfortable silence had settled in. She bent down to retrieve a bright orange sock from the floor by her bed. "I hope I'm bringing the right kind of clothes with me. I decided on jeans and sweatshirts and things like that. Was I right?"

Marcia got up and walked over to Jennifer's dresser where she slowly examined Jennifer's knickknacks one after another. "I don't think it matters much what you wear," Marcia said.

"That's what I said," Kate put in. "As long as she's comfortable, right?"

Instead of answering, Marcia picked up the little school picture of Mark that Jennifer had had framed. "Who's this?" she asked.

"That's Jennifer's boyfriend," Kate answered for Jennifer.

"Mmm," Marcia said thoughtfully. "He's kind of cute."

"Kind of cute!" cried Kate. "Mark's just the best looking guy in our entire school."

Marcia set the picture down and smiled a smile that could only be called indulgent.

"So what's the weather like on the island?" Jennifer asked, hoping to change the subject.

Marcia shrugged. "You know that it's off the coast of Canada, right? It can get cold, but I've been up there when it's been pretty warm, you know, warm enough to swim. It can rain a lot, too."

"What do you do up there mostly?" Jennifer asked, starting to lay clothes in her suitcase. "Fish?"

"The only fishing *I* do is for boys," Marcia said, loosening up and laughing a little. "And the biggest catch on the island is Peer Finstad. Unfortunately for you, he's already been caught."

"Peer Finstad?" Jennifer repeated, remembering the name her uncle had mentioned earlier. "He's your caretaker's son, isn't he?" She couldn't imagine her cousin—who seemed so formal and a bit snobby—being interested in a boy who worked for her family.

Marcia nodded. "That's right."

"How old is he?" Kate asked.

"Sixteen," Marcia answered, smiling dreamily. "Sweet sixteen."

"And he's already engaged?" Kate wondered.

"No, silly," Marcia scoffed. "Whatever gave you that idea?"

"I don't know. You said he'd been caught, and I thought—" Kate began.

"What I meant was that Peer is mine, all mine." Marcia smiled. "I'm the *only* person he's interested in."

"Doesn't he have any other friends?" Kate asked. Jennifer was wondering the same thing.

Marcia shook her head. "There aren't many other people on the island. His older brothers are his best friends, but they're working at a logging camp for the summer. Poor Peer. It's really hard on him when I'm away." Jennifer and Kate exchanged glances. Kate raised her eyebrows but neither girl said anything.

"Don't you just hate this suit?" Marcia suddenly asked, taking off her silk jacket and dropping it carelessly on the floor.

11

Jennifer shook her head. "I think it's beautiful."

Marcia sighed and said, "I'd give it to you in a minute, but my mother would have a fit. She insisted I have it for traveling. But that's how Mother is. *Everything* requires a different outfit—and nothing as casual as *jeans*." Marcia moved from Jennifer's dresser over to the closet.

"Sometimes I wish I could just dress like you do," she said, with a sigh. She looked Jennifer up and down.

"You must be exhausted from traveling. Maybe you'd like to freshen up?" Jennifer asked after another uncomfortable silence.

"I do feel kind of wilted," Marcia admitted.

"The bathroom is down the hall on the right," Jennifer told her cousin.

Marcia picked up the smaller of her two matching mustard-colored suitcases and sauntered out of the room. As soon as she was gone, Jennifer felt a flood of relief. How, she wondered, was she going to be able to stand her cousin for an entire month? All the excitement she'd been feeling at the thought of getting away without her parents was being replaced by a growing feeling of dread.

"Well, here's your going away present," Kate said as soon as they were alone. She pulled a gaily wrapped package from beneath the pillow on the guest bed, and handed it to Jennifer. "I was going to give it to you later, but I think I'd better let you have it while your cousin is 'freshening up'."

Jennifer tore open the package. It was a red notebook. Opening the cover, Jennifer saw that on the first page Kate had written, "Jennifer's Journal."

"A journal!" Jennifer cried. "Thanks!"

"It's not really just a journal, either! I got one for myself, too. I thought that we could both write down everything that happens during the next month, you know, everything we do and think. Then, when you get back, we'll trade. It'll almost be like we've been in two places at once that way." Kate smiled triumphantly.

Jennifer returned Kate's smile. "What a great idea! Sort of like a long letter that we never have to mail!"

Kate nodded. "Right!" Then Kate's smile faded as she said, "You don't seem as excited about going as you were before Marcia got here."

"Well . . . she's not exactly what I expected—whatever *that* was." Jennifer slipped the journal into her suitcase. Then she looked up at Kate and shrugged.

"Poor Jennifer," Kate said. "How are you going to put up with that attitude of hers for a whole month?"

Jennifer said, "Maybe Marcia isn't as bad as

she seems. Maybe she's just nervous or some-thing."

"Maybe," Kate said, "but I wouldn't count on it if I were you."

"Oh, well," Jennifer sighed. "It'll still be fun seeing the island and besides," Jennifer patted the red notebook, "I've got this journal and all the books you lent me. And," she added with a giggle, "who knows? Maybe I'll even do a little fishing."

"I hope you're right about all this," Kate said. "Because if you're not, it could be one of the longest months of your life."

Chapter Two

The next morning, Jennifer's parents stood by the front door with their arms around each other. Jennifer thought they looked sad, almost as sad as she felt. Jennifer was glad to have the chance to travel, but she knew she was going to miss her parents. She'd never really been away from home before. And Kate had said she'd come over to say goodbye, but, so far, she hadn't shown up.

"Isn't it time we got going?" Marcia asked, a little annoyed. The car was all packed. Everyone was more than ready.

"Just one more minute," Jennifer pleaded. "Kate's probably on her way over right now. Or maybe I should run over there."

"It doesn't look like anyone is up yet at the

McCluskys'," Mr. Garret pointed out. "And you did say goodbye to Kate last night. . . ."

"Your father is right," said Uncle Ben cheerfully. "We really ought to go. We don't want to miss our connections in Canada."

Reluctantly, Jennifer said, "Okay, then. I'm ready. Tell Kate I tried to wait, will you, Mom?" Mrs. Garrett nodded.

"Behave yourself," Mr. Garrett said, giving Jennifer a big hug and a kiss.

Then it was her mother's turn. "Have fun, honey. I'm glad you have this chance to go away, but—I'll miss you."

"I'll miss you too." Jennifer hugged her mother back. "I'll write," she said. "I promise."

Marcia rolled her eyes and climbed into the car. Then Uncle Ben and Jennifer followed her into the car and they were on their way.

Jennifer felt a lump in her throat as they pulled out of the driveway. She looked back and saw her mother and father, still standing in the doorway, waving. Jennifer had been so anxious to get away and have an adventure, but now she was having second thoughts.

"We're finally getting you out of this little town, Jennifer Garrett," Uncle Ben said as if he'd read her mind.

"Oh, Daddy," Marcia groaned. "You make it sound like we're taking Jennifer someplace exotic instead of even further into the wilderness where there's *nothing* to do."

"Now, now," Uncle Ben said, "the island is exotic in its own way. I'm sure Jennifer will love it."

"I'm sure I will," Jennifer agreed, even though she was already feeling the first pangs of homesickness. *I'm going to be more on my own than I've ever been before*, she told herself, already missing her parents and Kate and Mark and all her other friends. Uncle Ben was going to be busy with his business associates, and Marcia was going to be busy with Peer. *I'll be all alone*, Jennifer thought. Suddenly she felt like crying but she couldn't let Marcia see how upset she was. She would just have to tough it out.

Just outside of town, they reached the airport where Ben's private plane was waiting for them. Jennifer began feeling more excited. She'd only been on an airplane once before, the time her family had gone to visit Marcia and her parents. They'd taken a big, commercial airliner then. This little plane of her uncle's promised to be much more of an adventure.

"Do you fly the plane yourself, Uncle Ben?" Jennifer asked as they watched the ground crew gas the plane and load their luggage.

"I can," Uncle Ben replied. "But I have a pilot. It's safer."

Soon they were settling into their seats. Jen-

17

nifer's heart skipped a beat as the plane lifted off the ground. The view from the small, six-passenger plane was amazing. "Look, Jennifer," Uncle Ben said, pointing out the window. "There's your street . . . and there's—"

"Home!" shouted Jennifer. She could see her house, perfect and tiny down below. She wondered, for a second, if her parents would know she was looking down at them. " 'Bye, house," she said as she gave a wistful wave. And then they flew up through the clouds.

"Who wants to play cards?" asked Uncie Ben.

"Not me," said Marcia. "I need a nap."

"How about gin rummy," Jennifer suggested. She and her uncle played while Marcia dozed until the plane finally began its descent.

"Are we on the island now?" Jennifer asked, excited.

"We're in International Falls," Uncle Ben explained as the plane touched the ground. "We'll drive to Fort Francis from here and take a boat to the island from there."

When the threesome had gotten off the plane and walked into the small terminal building, Uncle Ben called out to a rugged-looking, dark-haired man in worn denims and a faded flannel shirt. "George! We're over here!"

"Well, Mr. Brewster, it's good to see you again," George Finstad said after he'd crossed the room. "The fishing has been extra fine the last couple of weeks. I think you're going to have a good time up here this summer."

"George, this is my niece, Jennifer Garrett. Jennifer, this is Mr. Finstad," Uncle Ben said.

"It's nice to meet you, Mr. Finstad," Jennifer said, shaking his big rough hand.

"Nice to meet you, too, Jennifer," he replied.

"And, of course, you remember my daughter Marcia," Uncle Ben said, stepping aside to reveal Marcia, who had been standing behind him.

"Hello there, Marcia," Mr. Finstad said. "You've grown up a bit, I see."

Marcia didn't reply. She only nodded a little, and gave Mr. Finstad a half-hearted smile.

"Where's Peer?" Uncle Ben asked as the group moved toward the cart which contained their luggage. Jennifer's ears perked up at the mention of her cousin's boyfriend. She was curious to see what sort of guy interested her cousin. So far, Marcia had seemed to shun everyone. *Peer must really be something!* Jennifer thought to herself.

"He's nearly grown up, Mr. Brewster—not content to trail after me anymore. In fact, today he's got a guide job of his own. Claims that's what he plans to do with the rest of his life."

Jennifer noted the pride in George Finstad's voice as he spoke of his son's plans. Then she tried to imagine Marcia living on a remote island, cleaning and frying fish for Peer and his clients. Jennifer stifled a giggle. *No way*, she thought. Marcia just wasn't the type. Jennifer was beginning to think that meeting Peer in itself would make the trip worthwhile.

Mr. Finstad picked up the handle of the cart and led the way out of the terminal.

"So, Peer is doing some guiding on his own this summer, is he? I only hope he's not showing someone else the choicest fishing spots," Uncle Ben said as they all walked to Finstad's van.

Jennifer heard Mr. Finstad chuckle. "He's smarter than that, Mr. Brewster. Anyway, even if he did, there's enough walleye this year for everyone. I guess that warm weather we had last summer gave the big fish plenty to feed on." He pulled open the van doors and began loading the luggage.

"I'll sit up front with George. I want to hear more about the fishing this summer," Uncle Ben told the girls. "You two can sit in the back and chat. Maybe you can point out some of the more notable sights to Jennifer, Marcia." As Uncle Ben turned to give George a hand, Marcia grimaced. *Marcia doesn't even seem to like her own father*, thought Jennifer. *Is there anyone she does like?*

"I don't know what he wants me to show you," said Marcia. "There isn't anything up here but *trees*."

"It's beautiful," Jennifer said, taking a deep breath and inhaling the fragrant scent of pine. "And it smells great," she added.

Marcia ignored her and climbed into the back seat of the van.

Jennifer sighed. Marcia's attitude was beginning to make her feel a little sour herself. *What's wrong with her*, Jennifer wondered. *Maybe she's upset about Peer. If he's spending all his time showing other people where to find fish, he probably won't have much time for Marcia.* Jennifer decided to try to get Marcia to open up.

"Don't worry, Marcia," Jennifer said once they were on the road. "Guiding probably doesn't take all of his time."

"All whose time?" Marcia asked, looking annoyed and baffled.

"Peer's, of course," Jennifer replied.

"Shh!" Marcia hissed, holding her finger fiercely to her lips. Then she nodded her head in the direction of Uncle Ben and George Finstad.

"What's wrong?" Jennifer asked. Marcia shook her head and scowled, making it clear that she wouldn't talk about Peer now.

"Oh," Jennifer said, "I get it." But, in fact, she really didn't get it. What was the big secret? Jennifer felt tired suddenly. She just wasn't in the mood to deal with Marcia's unfriendliness anymore—not for a while anyway.

Settling back in her seat, Jennifer looked out the window and tried to imagine what Peer must be like. He must be very special to have caught the attention of her very aloof cousin, Jennifer thought. Undoubtedly, he was dark like his father. If he spent all his time outside, he was probably very tan and rugged looking as well. Then her thoughts turned to her own boyfriend, Mark Brodie.

Mark was blond and blue-eyed, probably the exact opposite of Marcia's boyfriend. By the time Jennifer got back home, he'd be even blonder and tan as well thanks to his job as a lifeguard at the pool. Jennifer was happy he'd found a job he was really excited about, even though, as Kate said, all the girls in town would be flirting with him. But Jennifer couldn't muster up any jealousy. Sometimes she worried that the reason she wasn't jealous was because, as much as she liked Mark, she didn't love him. They had been such good friends for so long— since they'd been in diapers, Kate always joked. But Jennifer felt there was something missing from their relationship.

Jennifer sighed and leaned her head against the window. The thick evergreen forest was so beautiful. She imagined how romantic it would be, walking hand in hand through this forest with a *really* special boy.

Jennifer was so lost in her thoughts that she

was surprised when the van came to a stop in a large, public parking lot.

"Here we are," Uncle Ben said, eagerly hopping out of the van.

"And there's Peer!" Mr. Finstad said. There was both surprise and joy in his voice. "Peer! We're over here, son!"

Jennifer craned her neck around the van trying to get a glimpse of the boy who had captivated her otherwise bored cousin Marcia. One look and she knew why even Marcia was moved by him.

"Is *that* Peer?" she whispered to Marcia.

Marcia was actually smiling. "Isn't he gorgeous?" she whispered back.

It was all Jennifer could do to nod in reply. Peer Finstad was the best looking boy, if you could call him a boy, she'd ever seen. He was at least six feet tall and quite muscular. His hair was jet black and he was wearing dark glasses. He had on basically the same clothes as his father, faded jeans, a faded flannel shirt and well-worn leather boots. He could just as easily have been a movie star, though, as a fishing guide.

"Hi, Dad," Peer said, joining them. He had an easy way of walking, loose and confident. "I had another great morning. We caught our limit so fast that I had my party drop me off here so I could give you a hand."

"You remember the Brewsters, don't you?" Mr. Finstad said.

Peer looked in their direction and flashed an amazing smile. Jennifer felt her knees get weak. "Hello, Mr. Brewster," Peer said, holding out his hand. Next, he looked from Marcia to Jennifer, then back at Marcia again. His smile vanished, and he seemed confused.

With a laugh, Uncle Ben said, "The girls do have a definite family resemblance, don't they, Peer?" Then he put his hand on Jennifer's shoulder. "This is my niece, Jennifer Garrett. I'm sure you remember Marcia."

Peer's ruddy cheeks darkened a little more in obvious embarrassment at the mix-up. He gave Marcia a nod and said, "Hi again, Marcia." Then he turned back to Jennifer and said, "Nice to meet you, Jennifer . . . or should I call you Jenny?"

"Whichever you prefer," Jennifer told him with a smile. She tried to see through Peer's dark glasses to the eyes behind them. But the silvery surface only reflected her own face back at her.

"*We* call her Jennifer," Marcia said shortly, snapping Jennifer out of her trance-like state.

What's wrong with her? Jennifer asked herself.

"But *I'd* prefer to call you Jenny," Peer said boldly. Slowly, he removed his dark glasses. His eyes were coal black, but sparkled with mischief. Jennifer knew she was going to have to be doubly careful. She could tell that Peer was clearly a boy who enjoyed teasing, and teasing was something that Jennifer was afraid Marcia wouldn't enjoy at all.

Jennifer looked down at her white leather sneakers. "Whatever," she said, grateful to discover her shoelace needed retying. She knelt down to tie her shoe and escape Peer's piercing eyes. The last thing Jennifer wanted or needed was to antagonize her already difficult cousin.

Jennifer was afraid to get up once her shoe was tied. What if Peer was still looking at her? Conversation was going on around her, but she was too busy trying to ignore Peer to pay much attention to it.

Suddenly it got quiet. Jennifer looked up, puzzled. Everyone had left her and was heading across the parking lot. Grabbing her suitcase, Jennifer ran to catch up with the others. Now that the uncomfortable moment had passed, Jennifer felt foolish for thinking that Peer had been flirting with her. She had probably just imagined it.

Then she realized that she hadn't imagined the way that Peer seemed to be completely ignoring Marcia. *Maybe they had a fight*, Jennifer thought. *Or maybe this is just an act because they don't want anyone to know there's anything between them. Anyway, it really isn't any of my business.* Jennifer caught up with the group as the last piece of luggage was loaded onto the boat. She handed her suitcase to Peer, and carefully not looking at him, climbed aboard. Soon they were speeding toward the island. The beautiful clear water of Rainy Lake sparkled in the late afternoon sun as their speed boat flew past island after island. A brisk wind blew Jennifer's long, dark hair away from her face as the boat cut through the water. Suddenly she was incredibly happy she'd come on this trip. Whatever else might happen, flying over the water was paradise. She felt free and ready for an adventure.

Jennifer tried to keep her mind on the scenery but, as the boat ride continued, she kept thinking of Peer. The sun shining on his black hair gave it a bluish sheen, like the hair of Superman in the comic books she used to read. *Cleverly disguised as a mild-mannered woodsman . . .* she thought to herself and laughed.

"What's so funny?" Marcia asked, peering curiously at Jennifer.

Jennifer briefly considered sharing her joke with Marcia, then quickly decided against it. Marcia wouldn't think it was funny. She'd probably be furious that Jennifer was thinking about Peer.

"Nothing, really. I'm just happy. This is *so* great," Jennifer said, gesturing to indicate the scenery, the boat, everything. Marcia rolled her eyes and shook her head as if to say Jennifer was more than a little goofy.

Jennifer looked to the right just as Peer steered the boat in that direction. Suddenly they were drawing toward the most beautiful island Jennifer had seen that day.

"Here we are," Uncle Ben shouted above the noise from the boat's engine. "This is it!"

First Jennifer took in the white two-story house which stood at the end of the long dock. Then she noticed that on both sides of the house there were stairs carved right into the rock! Letting her eyes follow the stairs, she saw that they each ended at two log cabins, a very large one on the left and a much smaller one on the right.

"The white house at the end of the dock is the Finstads' house," Uncle Ben said when Jennifer looked at him and smiled. "You and Marcia will be staying in the smaller log cabin. I'll be in the larger cabin so I can host the clients I plan to entertain up here this month."

"We're going to be in our own cabin?" Jennifer asked, hearing the alarm in her own voice. "Just Marcia and me?" Jennifer stole a quick glance at Marcia and tried to imagine what being in a cabin alone with her for a whole month was going to be like. They'd been together less than twenty-four hours and already they'd run out of things to say to each other.

Uncle Ben chuckled. "It's a private island, remember. There's no one on the island but us. You'll be perfectly safe," he told her, misunderstanding her reason for alarm. "Besides, the Finstads' place is just a stone's throw away."

"It's all *very* cozy," Marcia assured her in a cold tone that was anything but cozy.

After Peer had landed the boat and tied it to the dock, his father said, "You give the girls a hand up to their cabin, Peer. I'll get Mr. Brewster settled on the hill."

"Okay, Dad," Peer said. He took off his sunglasses again and slipped them into his shirt pocket. Somehow, he managed to pick up both of Marcia's suitcases and Jennifer's bag as well. "Come on, girls," he said with a smile. Then the three of them were on their way up the hill to the smaller cabin, Peer striding ahead and Jennifer bringing up the rear.

Chapter Three

"There you go," Peer said cheerfully, setting their suitcases inside the cabin door. "Mom's got everything made up for you, I'm sure. But if you need anything . . . Well, you know the routine, don't you, Marcia?"

Marcia nodded. "I ought to by now," she said. "In fact, I think of this as my home."

Peer drew his dark brows together in a scowl that surprised Jennifer. "You don't need to rub it in, you know. I got the picture a long time ago." Then he turned and stomped out, the screen door slamming behind him.

"What was all that about?" Jennifer asked. Peer seemed to go from pleasant to angry at the drop of a hat. Was everyone crazy, she wondered, or was it her?

"Nothing," Marcia assured her calmly. "It's just that he doesn't know you know about us, that's all. He was obviously putting on a show for your benefit. You see, our families don't know how we feel about each other and if they did . . . Well, I'm sure you see the problem."

Jennifer shook her head. She had no idea what the problem could be. Neither father seemed to be trying to keep Marcia and Peer apart.

But when Jennifer told Marcia that, her cousin merely laughed. "You're kind of dense, aren't you? The reason they don't try to keep us apart is obvious. They don't think they *have* to. Peer makes sure they think we don't even *like* each other. So, actually, that's why you're here."

"It is?" Jennifer said.

"You're here as my hired playmate, to keep me from being lonely and getting bored," Marcia said. "Your mother must have told you. My father told me in so many words that that was what was going on."

Jennifer stared at her cousin. "I know my mother wanted me to come. But all she said was that she hoped we'd get to be like sisters. She thinks being an only child is difficult," Jennifer told her, hurt by Marcia's blunt words. Coming to the island and getting to know her cousin better had seemed an appealing idea at the time, but now her mother's words seemed almost silly.

"My mother doesn't like only children either," Marcia said with a wry smile. "That's why she thinks I should never have been born."

"Your mother actually *said* that?" Jennifer asked, feeling shocked and suddenly very sorry for her cousin.

Marcia nodded. "She says it all the time. Why do you think she isn't here now? Of course, part of the reason is that she isn't all that fond of Daddy either."

"I can't imagine a mother feeling that way," Jennifer said quickly. "I'm sure she really loves you."

"You're so naive. But I'm used to it by now, if you really want to know. I've had fifteen years of taking care of myself, and I really like my independence. I certainly don't need you around. But I guess we'll have to tolerate each other. Then maybe we can both have a little fun while we're here."

Jennifer didn't like Marcia's tone of voice. Yet something held her back from telling Marcia off. Despite her fancy clothes and many travels, Marcia seemed to be very unhappy. Maybe that was why she was so obnoxious. Jennifer figured the best thing to do was hear Marcia out and try to get to understand her a little better.

After all, they were going to be together for a whole month.

"I'm interested in having fun," Jennifer agreed.

"Okay. Come on. I'll show you around." Marcia led the way into a second room, nearly as large as the living room. "This is the bedroom."

The room had a rustic look. The two double beds and the nightstands next to them as well as two chairs and the table which stood between them were all made of highly varnished pine. The beds were covered with brightly colored, hand-made patchwork quilts. There were two large windows, one of which looked out on the woods while the other looked out on the water. In Jennifer's opinion, the room was a dream come true.

"Oh," Jennifer cried. "This is lovely!"

"It's also mine. I've always had this room as my bedroom. I'm sure you understand." Marcia set the larger of her two suitcases down on one of the beds. Then she opened it and started taking things out carefully.

Jennifer just stood looking at her. The room was clearly large enough for both of them. Finally she said, "Is there another bedroom then?"

Marcia looked up and shook her head. "No. But you can have the loft to yourself." She motioned Jennifer toward the living room, the gesture full of impatience. Without waiting for

Marcia to say more, Jennifer picked up her suitcase and headed for the living room.

When she got to the living room, Jennifer saw the loft she'd missed before. It hung over the little eating area adjacent to the kitchen. Jennifer could see that it had an excellent view of the large, stone fireplace that covered the entire wall opposite it. It was wonderful.

Marcia could have the large bedroom all to herself, Jennifer thought. She'd be more than happy to be in the cozy little loft. One of Jennifer's favorite fantasies was to have a bedroom with a fireplace in it so she could fall asleep gazing at the flames. It seemed so old-fashioned and romantic. The loft would suit her well.

Jennifer dragged her heavy suitcase up the ladder of the loft. Plunking herself down on the cot, Jennifer reached into her suitcase and pulled out her journal. She immediately felt as if Kate was sitting right there on the bed with her. "Dear Kate," she wrote along the top of the page. "You would not believe this place! It's simply—"

"Hey," Marcia said, starting up the ladder. "Need sheets?"

Jennifer quickly closed her journal. "Yes," she said, checking under the heavy wool blanket and finding a bare mattress. "I guess I do. Are there sheets for this cot downstairs?"

Marcia tossed a set of white flannel sheets

onto the floor of the loft next to the bed. "I found these for you."

"Flannel!" Jennifer cried. "I just love flannel sheets!"

"Good," Marcia said, "because that's all I could find."

"Come on up," Jennifer said. Maybe if she pretended Marcia was Kate, they'd get along better. "We can talk while I make my bed."

Marcia paused for a moment, then climbed the rest of the way into the loft. "I've never been up here before," she confessed, taking a seat in a little wicker rocking chair that was in the corner.

"You haven't? Gosh," Jennifer said, "even if I wasn't sleeping up here, I'd want to come up here." She looked up at the round pine beams of the roof. "It's so cozy!" she said.

"You must be quite a reader," Marcia said, taking in the paperbacks Jennifer had neatly stacked on the little bedside table.

"Actually, I don't read as much as Kate does. But, you know, I feel as if I do because Kate is always telling me the plots of all the stuff she reads!" Jennifer stood up. She pulled the blanket off the cot and began putting on the fitted bottom sheet. Then she shook out the top sheet and neatly folded the corners under the mattress. Finally, she returned the thick wool blanket with its bold stripes of red, yellow and green to the bed.

"You're pretty good at that," Marcia said.

"It's just making a bed," Jennifer said with a shrug, though pleased with her cousin's compliment. "I mean, I do it all the time at home."

"That's something I never do. Someone always does it for me," Marcia said. "Not that I mind!" The two girls shared a grin that was cut short by the sound of the door opening.

"Girls!" It was Uncle Ben. "Where are you?"

"We're up here, Uncle Ben," Jennifer called back.

Jennifer listened to her uncle clomp across the living room. Then, catching sight of them in the loft, he asked, "What are you doing up there?"

"Jennifer has insisted on sleeping up here, Daddy," Marcia said quickly.

"Wha—?" Jennifer began.

"But there are two perfectly good beds in the bedroom," Uncle Ben said, scowling. "I thought it would be nice for you two to be together." Jennifer thought her uncle sounded disappointed and was annoyed that he believed she was responsible for the setup.

"I know that," Marcia said, a faint whine to her voice. She got to her feet and started down the ladder. "But Jennifer is a guest, and I

35

thought . . ." She let her voice trail off into a resigned sigh.

"You were right," Uncle Ben assured her, but not before giving Jennifer a disappointed look. "That was very thoughtful of you, Marcia."

How unfair! Jennifer thought to herself. Uncle Ben thought *she* was the one that was being unfriendly. Yet trying to explain what had really happened would only create an awkward situation with both her uncle and her cousin, Jennifer was certain. Besides, now that she was settled in the loft, it really was where she preferred to stay.

Jennifer started down the ladder. "I could make us some dinner," she offered, hoping that her willingness to help would redeem her in her uncle's eyes.

"Heavens no!" Uncle Ben said.

"Darlene Finstad does all the cooking," Marcia explained, her tone implying that Jennifer was a fool for not having realized that herself.

"In fact, dinner is all ready down at my cabin. Come along now, you two. I guess I'd better tell Darlene that you'll be sleeping in the loft so she can make up a bed for you," Uncle Ben said, heading toward the door.

"I already made the bed up myself," Jennifer said. "Marcia found sheets."

"My, aren't you the independent one," said

Uncle Ben. But the *way* he said it left Jennifer doubting that he was paying her a compliment.

"You two go along," Marcia said, heading for the bathroom. "I'll catch up with you."

"So," Uncle Ben said as he followed Jennifer down the path toward his cabin, "I hope you and Marcia are finding some common ground."

Jennifer thought of the brief exchange she'd shared with her cousin in the loft just before her uncle had arrived and interrupted them. It hadn't been exactly warm, but it was something. Maybe the two of them being alone in their own cabin would work out after all.

Jennifer was still trying to decide how to answer her uncle's question, when Marcia caught up with them. Jennifer couldn't help noticing that her cousin looked stunning.

When the three of them reached the larger cabin, it was as if elves had been there ahead of them. There was a roaring fire in the enormous stone fireplace and candles burning brightly on the large dining table. Three places were set at one end of the table, and the fish—fresh walleye caught by Peer that morning, Uncle Ben told Jennifer—boiled potatoes and creamed peas were all steaming hot. Yet, there was no one in sight to take credit for their comfort.

As they ate, Uncle Ben asked Jennifer questions about his sister and the town where he'd grown up. Jennifer wanted to contribute more than the short answers she was giving, but she was so tired that she was afraid that if she didn't go to bed soon, she'd fall asleep right there at the table.

"My goodness," Uncle Ben said when Jennifer yawned for the fourth time. "I think we're losing someone."

"It was a long, exciting day," Jennifer admitted, pausing to yawn again. "I'll just help with the dishes, then I'll go to bed."

"Darlene does the dishes," Uncle Ben said, looking amused. "You girls run along. There's a flashlight on the hook by the door. Take that so you don't stumble on the rock steps."

"Oh, Marcia doesn't need to come with me, if she doesn't want to," Jennifer assured him. "I can get back by myself." She pointed out the large picture window that afforded a magnificent view of the lake which was bathed in the light of a nearly full moon. "I don't even think I need a flashlight."

"I'm tired, too," Marcia said, getting to her feet. "I'll go with you."

"Take the flashlight," Uncle Ben said, giving it to Marcia. "You can bring it back tomorrow."

When the girls got back to their own cabin, they found Peer on his knees in front of the fireplace. He was about to put a match to a large stack of carefully placed wood.

"Oh, a fire!" Jennifer cried, delighted. "What a nice surprise!"

Without turning around, Peer said, "Hi. Didn't Marcia tell you that you get a fire in here every night? I also brought brownies that Mom baked today for your dessert."

The walk through the crisp night air had revived Jennifer a little bit. Seeing Peer had revived her even more. She was anxious for him to know that she knew about his relationship with Marcia. She hoped that would put him at ease and the three of them could get on with becoming friends.

"You look like an expert at building fires," Jennifer ventured.

"I should be," Peer said as the match caught and the fire burst to life. "I've been doing this since I was old enough to hold a match without burning myself. But thanks." He stood up and smiled at Jennifer as he dusted off his jeans.

Marcia sauntered across the living room and sat down on the edge of the couch just a few inches away from where Peer was standing. "Oh, brownies! They really look good."

"Of course they do," said Peer. "My mother is a terrific cook, the best in all of Ontario."

"She certainly made us a good dinner," Jennifer said. She sat down on a chair facing the couch. "But I guess we ought to thank you for that, too. Uncle Ben said we were eating the fish you caught today."

"You'll be eating your own fish soon," Peer promised.

"I've never really fished before," Jennifer confessed. "Do you think I'll be able to learn?"

"There's not much to it," Marcia said. "You just drop a line in the water, wait, and bang! You've got a fish!"

Peer laughed. "That's the way *you* fish, Marcia, because you've always had a Finstad to bait your hook and take you where the fish are biting. If I remember correctly, you've always had someone else take the fish off the hook as well."

Marcia's blue eyes clouded and her body seemed to stiffen. "I've been fishing for years."

Peer nodded. "Every summer that I can remember, you've been here, all right. This is your father's island, but neither you nor your father would have much fun without us here to look after you."

Marcia's scowl melted into a smile. "You're right about that. I wouldn't even want to be here if *you* weren't here. Won't you sit down and have a brownie with us?"

Peer shook his head. "We've got some back at the house. Anyway, you both must be beat after your long trip today, and I've got to get up before dawn."

40

"Will you be taking us fishing in the morning?" Jennifer asked.

Peer shook his head. "I've got another job in the morning, but I'll take you girls out in the afternoon if you want."

Peer started toward the back door, but before he could open it, Marcia called him back. "Don't go," she said. Her voice sounded meek, like a little girl who was afraid of the dark.

"What is it? Do you want something else?" he asked. Jennifer knew exactly what Marcia wanted. She wanted Peer. Jennifer felt she should tell Peer not to worry, that she knew what was going on between Peer and Marcia. But wasn't it Marcia's place to speak up? Jennifer wasn't sure what to do.

"What's your rush?" Marcia asked. She picked up a brownie and took a bite. "Have just one brownie with us. Tell us about the job you're going on in the morning."

Peer took a step backward, then said, "No. Thank you, but I really can't. Dad's got another chore for me tonight."

"Please," Marcia pleaded again.

Peer reached behind his back and took hold of the doorknob. As he opened the door, he said, "I really can't. Maybe some other time."

"I wish you'd just told him that I know about you two," Jennifer said, closing the door behind Peer. "It's silly to carry on this charade for no reason."

Marcia tossed the brownie she'd been holding back onto the plate. "You just don't understand anything, do you?" She shot Jennifer a withering look. Then she stood up and stomped to the bedroom, slamming the door shut.

"B-but . . ." Jennifer stammered, staring at the closed door. She was stunned by Marcia's anger. What had she done?

Something odd was going on, Jennifer was sure of that much. She was also sure she wanted no part of it. From the looks of things, both Peer and Marcia were playing an unpleasant game with each other, a game it seemed no one could possibly win.

Oh, well, Jennifer told herself, she wasn't going to let it ruin her evening. The fire burned merrily, and the brownies were delicious. Jennifer took a second brownie and curled up on the couch, staring into the hypnotic flames. It was a relief to finally be alone.

Chapter Four

Jennifer opened her eyes the next morning, not quite certain where she was. Then she saw the cabin's rafters above her head and remembered she was on her Uncle Ben's island in Canada.

Looking over the railing of the loft toward the window, Jennifer saw the early morning sun sparkling on the lake. She threw back the covers and sat up. But the sunshine outside was misleading. It was cold! She burrowed back under the covers.

As Jennifer was trying to decide whether or not to get up, she saw Marcia tiptoe out of the bedroom and steal across the living room. Her dark hair was loose and looked shiny and full, as if she had just washed and dried it. She was wearing skin-tight black designer jeans and an oversized red sweater, and baggy red socks with high-top black sneakers.

Marcia disappeared from view as she continued to tiptoe under the loft. Then Jennifer heard the door slowly open and close again. Marcia had left without a word, but Jennifer didn't mind. She suspected that Marcia was sneaking off for a rendezvous with Peer, and she had the feeling that the sooner those two got back on track, the better it was going to be for everyone.

Jennifer decided it was time she got dressed. She didn't have a sophisticated outfit like Marcia's. Her blue jeans and pink-and-black-checked flannel shirt would just have to do. She tied back her hair with a pink bow and then slipped into her flannel lined denim jacket.

As she started down the loft ladder with her journal, Jennifer realized she was very hungry. She went to the kitchen to see if there was anything to eat in the cabin.

Thankfully, the kitchen was well-stocked. Jennifer found milk and butter and fresh fruit in the refrigerator. A loaf of homemade bread was in a wooden breadbox on the counter by the sink, and there were several boxes of unopened cereal in the cupboard.

Jennifer toasted some bread and sat down at the table. She was buttering her toast when the back door opened. Jennifer turned, expecting to see Marcia. But it was Uncle Ben.

"Jennifer!" he said, sounding surprised. "You *are* up!"

"Good morning, Uncle Ben," Jennifer said. "I just got up a little bit ago. Isn't it a beautiful morning!"

"It's more like a beautiful afternoon. I've been up for hours myself. I've even got a stringer of fish waiting to be cleaned at the fish house to prove it," Uncle Ben told her. Then he looked at the food she was fixing herself. "But what are you doing?"

Jennifer looked down at her toast. Wasn't it obvious what she was doing? she wondered. But she said, "I'm having breakfast. Want to join me?"

"Darlene has a *brunch* all ready for us at the big cabin. That's why I'm here. To bring you down."

"Oh," Jennifer said, feeling suddenly awkward. "I didn't know that." She gestured at the food she'd laid out. "I mean, no one ever told me. . . ."

"Don't worry about it," Uncle Ben said, giving her hand a reassuring pat. "But I want you to eat with us. Marcia's down there waiting for us."

Marcia? Jennifer was sure that her cousin

45

had gone to meet Peer. The whole situation was getting more confusing and frustrating by the minute! Why, she wondered, hadn't Marcia said something to her instead of sneaking out if she was only going to her father's cabin for breakfast? What kind of trick was Marcia trying to pull?

"I'll just clean this up, and then I'll come down," Jennifer told her uncle.

"Darlene can take care of all this later," Uncle Ben said, shooing her toward the door. "Come along now, or everything will be cold. You don't want to hurt Darlene's feelings, do you?"

Jennifer looked helplessly at her Uncle Ben. She wanted to explain things to him so that he'd know that all she wanted was for everyone to be happy. Jennifer wanted to let her uncle know that she wasn't at all the difficult loner he seemed to think she was.

"There you are!" Marcia said as Jennifer stepped into the larger cabin behind her uncle. "I thought you might sleep all day."

"Hi," Jennifer said, sitting down at the same place she'd sat at dinner the night before. "What time is it anyway?"

"It's nearly nine o'clock," a woman's voice called from the kitchen. Jennifer knew the voice had to belong to Mrs. Finstad.

Jennifer stifled a yawn. "I thought it must

be almost noon by the way you were talking, Uncle Ben."

"Nine o'clock is late around here," Uncle Ben said, joining the girls at the table. "This is fishing country, remember? You have to get up with the fish if you want to catch them."

"Well put, Mr. Brewster," Mrs. Finstad said, coming into the dining room with a platter full of pancakes bursting with blueberries in one hand and a platter of thick sliced bacon in the other. She was a large, handsome woman who had the same dark, penetrating eyes as Peer.

"I'm already done with my breakfast," Marcia announced before Mrs. Brewster had even set the platters on the table.

Uncle Ben looked at Marcia's plate. Then he looked at Marcia. "What was this breakfast?"

"Coffee," she replied, getting to her feet. "Some orange juice and a couple of pancakes."

Mrs. Finstad smiled. "Marcia ate my griddle warmers. I usually just toss those out. But she insisted."

"Like you said, Dad, it's late, and I promised Peer I'd help him with his errands." Marcia flicked her hair behind her back. Marcia looked as if she was ready for a day of heavy shopping instead of a day of fishing, Jennifer thought.

"Oh," Marcia said, her face breaking into a triumphant smile, "here's Peer now!"

"Where are your errands going to take you?"
Uncle Ben asked when Peer stood in the cabin's
doorway.

"Back to town. The motor on the small boat
is acting up again," Peer said. "Dad thinks he
can fix it, though, if I can find a spare part."

Uncle Ben speared several of the steaming
pancakes with the serving fork. Then he handed
the fork to Jennifer. "Hurry up, Jennifer. I'm
sure the kids will wait for you."

Jennifer glanced at Marcia and knew immediately that she wasn't welcome on this particu-
lar errand. "I think I'll stay here," she said as
she carefully put a couple of pancakes on her own
plate. It was clear to her that Peer and Marcia
needed some time alone together. Jennifer was
more than ready to give it to them, too.

"The town isn't going to disappear in ten
minutes," Peer assured Jennifer. "We'll wait for
you. You *do* want to go for a boat ride, don't
you?"

Was he asking her along as an act for the
benefit of Uncle Ben and his mother? Jennifer
wondered. Had Marcia finally told him that Jennifer knew about their relationship? She searched
his dark eyes for a clue to what he was thinking, but Peer was too difficult for her to read.

"Come on, everyone. Leave the poor girl alone,"
Marcia said, as if she were protecting Jennifer

48

from the others. "Jennifer said she didn't want to come. Let's let her do what she wants. She's our guest, isn't she?"

Uncle Ben chuckled. "You're right, baby. Go on then, you two. I can entertain Jennifer."

"I don't need to be entertained," Jennifer said firmly as the door shut behind Marcia and Peer. "I have plenty of things to do to keep me busy."

"So," Uncle Ben said, passing Jennifer the platter of bacon. "What are all these thing you have to do?"

Jennifer took some bacon and another pancake and began to butter it. "Well, I can go walking and swimming. And I've brought quite a few books with me," she said. She didn't want to tell her uncle about the journal Kate had given her.

"You're a reader then," Uncle Ben said, making it sound like a defect of some sort.

Jennifer shrugged. "I guess you could say that." She'd never thought of herself as a reader before. Kate was the bookworm. But she guessed she was going to be a reader by the end of the month, especially if Marcia and Peer kept dashing off without her.

"I'll leave you to your reading then," Uncle Ben said, getting to his feet. "I'm going to see if I can remember how to fillet a walleye."

"Have fun," Jennifer called after him.

As soon as Uncle Ben had left the cabin, Jennifer gathered up the breakfast dishes and brought them to the kitchen where Mrs. Finstad was elbow deep in dishwater.

"I'll dry," Jennifer said, picking up the dish towel from the counter.

"Aren't you a nice girl!" Mrs. Finstad said, smiling. "But you don't need to do that. You're on vacation, after all. Go on and enjoy yourself."

"I want to help," Jennifer assured her. "I'm not used to being waited on. You know," she added, picking up a handful of silver and drying it, "it kind of makes me nervous."

Mrs. Finstad chuckled. "I'm the same way myself. I can't stand to sit. Well, some of us are doers and some of us are sitters, I guess."

After the dishes were done, Jennifer helped Mrs. Finstad with the beds, first in Ben's cabin and then in the girls' cabin. The older woman seemed to have a saying for everything, reminding Jennifer of her mother and making her feel right at home.

When they'd finished with the kitchen in the smaller cabin, Jennifer said, "I guess I'll go explore the woods."

Mrs. Finstad nodded. "Should have warmed up into a pleasant day by now," she said. "My boys have worn several paths all over this island. It's a surprisingly big island. But you'll see all that for yourself, I guess. Have fun."

"Thank you," Jennifer said. She picked her journal up from the kitchen counter. Then, tucking it under her arm, she strolled out the back door.

As soon as Jennifer was outside, she noticed that there was indeed a path leading from the cabin into the woods. The sunlight filtered through the trees, creating interesting shadows, and she could smell the effect of the warmth on the pine needles that covered the ground. Helping Mrs. Finstad and chatting with her had restored Jennifer's peace of mind. She began humming to herself as she strolled.

It wasn't long before Jennifer was deep in the woods. She could still hear the hum of distant boat motors, but she couldn't see the water that had seemed like such an overwhelming presence back at the cabins. Jennifer loved water, the way the sun danced on its surface, the noise it made as it lapped the rocky shore. But, at the moment, she was enjoying the feeling of being completely enclosed by the forest.

Suddenly, Jennifer found herself in a clearing. A few tree stumps told her that this clearing was man made. Then she spotted a circle of stones that she immediately recognized as a fire scar. Several other trails seemed to converge in the clearing.

"You've found my secret spot," someone said.

Jennifer dropped her notebook and spun around. It was Peer, and he was alone! "Not many of the guests ever come back in here. In fact, you may be the first."

"I'm sorry," she said, clutching her notebook.

"Don't be sorry. I don't really mind. Anyway, it wouldn't matter if I did. This island belongs to the Brewsters, not the Finstads." Peer smiled at her. He wasn't wearing his sunglasses and Jennifer noted that his eyelashes were long and thick.

"Oh, I don't know," Jennifer mused. "It seems to me that your family owns this island at least as much as my uncle does. I mean, he only comes here once in a while. You guys live here all the time. Isn't there some saying about possession being nine tenths of the law or something?"

Peer laughed. "I find myself thinking that way sometimes. But deep inside I know it isn't true. Anyway, you came here for a reason, and I'm probably keeping you from whatever it is."

"Not at all," Jennifer said. "I was just going for a walk. You did surprise me, though. I thought you'd gone to the mainland and didn't expect you to be back this soon."

"I did go to the mainland. I just grabbed the part I needed at the hardware store and came right back, though. I've been back a while." He

52

laughed again. "About long enough to stop your uncle from totally butchering all the fish he caught this morning. He's got two fillets reasonably intact at least. The rest of his efforts will make a good fish chowder. My mother will see to that."

Jennifer couldn't help smiling. "Is he really that bad?" she asked mischieviously.

Peer stopped smiling. "Hey," he said, "don't get me wrong. I like your uncle. He's a good man."

"I know," Jennifer agreed. "I like him too. But he talks like he's such a great fisherman. You should have heard the fish stories he was telling my dad while he was at our house."

"Well, we can't expect him to be as good as my father. After all, my dad is a professional fisherman," Peer told her.

"So are you, aren't you?" Jennifer asked.

Peer nodded thoughtfully. "Yes, I guess I am! I love it here. I've got two older brothers, you know. They couldn't wait to get away. But not me. I hope to stay in these parts all my life, doing just what my father does."

"I can sure understand what would make you feel that way," Jennifer told him. "It's so beautiful here! I love the smell of these pine trees."

"They're all different, you know. Most people don't seem to notice that. Over there," Peer said, "that's a white pine. And that one is a red pine. That's a spruce, and the little one is a balsam fir."

"Those are birch trees, aren't they?" Jennifer asked.

Peer nodded. "Yup. But one's a white birch and one's a yellow birch."

"I'm not sure I can remember all that," Jennifer confessed. "But I'm impressed."

"Come here," Peer said, motioning Jennifer to follow him. "I want to share something special with you." Jennifer followed Peer to the edge of the clearing.

"See this?" Peer said, pointing at a large boulder. Jennifer nodded. It looked just like one of hundreds of such boulders in the area.

"Don't tell me this rock has a special name or something," Jennifer teased.

"This," Peer told her, patting the rock lovingly, "is a natural rock chair. Go on," he urged, "try it out."

Carefully, Jennifer climbed up to the top of the boulder. It didn't look much like a chair, but Jennifer didn't want Peer to think she was a poor sport for refusing to try it out. As she turned around to sit down, however, she found that there was an indentation like a pocket. She leaned back and discovered that it was like sitting in a bean bag chair.

"Hey, this is great!" she cried. She snuggled

into the space a little more. "I never would have thought a rock could be so comfortable!"

Peer smiled. "Now you've got a place to sit while you write," he said, nodding at the notebook she was still clutching.

Jennifer had forgotten about her journal. Blushing, she said, "Thank you."

"Don't mention it. Well, I've got to go back. Dad's probably looking for me to give him a hand with that engine. Are we still on for fishing later?" he asked.

"I don't know," Jennifer said hesitantly. She did want to go fishing, but she didn't want Marcia to misinterpret her friendliness with Peer. Arousing Marcia's jealousy wasn't part of Jennifer's plans for the month.

"Oh," said Peer. He took a step backward, as if he suddenly understood something that had been unclear before. "Well, let me know when you know, okay?" With that, he turned and stalked off down one of the paths Jennifer had yet to try.

Jennifer kept looking down the path long after he was gone. He'd been so friendly and so easy for her to talk to. But, when he'd left, he had seemed upset or put out about something. What, she wondered, had she done to offend *him*?

Sighing, she opened the red notebook. She reread the entry she'd completed earlier where she'd described the trip and island to Kate.

Then she began her second entry. "Dear Kate," she wrote, "Peer Finstad is really a special boy. I think he and I could be friends. But I'm going to have to be careful. I'm not at all sure that Marcia would approve of such a friendship, and if I get on her wrong side too early in the month, life is going to be miserable for me."

Chapter Five

Once Jennifer had finished her entry, she closed her journal and started back to the cabin. Just as she reached the door, Marcia came flying out.

"There you are!" Marcia said. "Everyone's been looking for you!"

"I was in the woods. I saw Peer a little while ago, though. Didn't he say he'd seen me?" Jennifer asked.

"Peer!" Marcia exclaimed. "What did you say to him? What did you talk about?"

Jennifer shrugged her shoulders. "Nothing really. We just talked about trees and rocks and things. Then he said he had to go help his father with the engine."

"You didn't mention me, did you?" Marcia demanded.

"No," Jennifer replied. "Your name never came up."

"Good. I still haven't told him that I talked to you about us. I don't think he'd understand. Not yet, anyway. Promise you won't say anything."

"Don't worry. I'm not sure what I'd say anyway," Jennifer told her. "But you said everyone was looking for me. What's up?"

"We're going fishing. Dad wanted to know if you wanted to come. Do you?" Marcia asked. She didn't seem too anxious for Jennifer to say yes. But Jennifer didn't care. She wanted to go fishing, and she was going to go!

"Sure! When?" she asked.

"Right now," Marcia said.

"Let me put this inside," Jennifer said, waving her red notebook at Marcia. "I'll be right out."

"I'll go on down to the dock and tell them to wait for you." With that, Marcia took off at a run.

Jennifer had a feeling that if she didn't get down to the dock as quickly as she could, Marcia would probably tell Uncle Ben she wasn't coming. Hurriedly, she tossed her notebook on the kitchen table, then turned and followed her cousin.

"Jennifer!" Uncle Ben cried as she neared the boat. "We were about to leave without you!"

Jennifer gave Marcia a cool look. Then she said to her uncle, "I wouldn't miss fishing for the world, Uncle Ben. After all, that's one of the main reasons I came on this trip."

"We're all set then," Mr. Finstad proclaimed. "As soon as Peer gets here, we'll shove off."

Jennifer looked toward the Finstads' house and saw Peer coming toward them, taking long strides that rattled the wooden planks of the dock. He was carrying two fishing rods completely set up with spinning reels and line.

When he reached the boat, he smiled at Jennifer. "I came looking for you, but I must have just missed you. I set up this rod for you on the chance that you'd decided to come after all," he added, handing her the sturdier looking of the two rods. Jennifer thanked him. Then Peer untied the boat and hopped in up front next to his father.

Marcia gave Jennifer a withering look. But Jennifer refused to let Marcia intimidate her. While she'd been writing in her journal, Jennifer had decided she'd be friendly with Peer. There was really no reason for her not to be—other than Marcia's petty jealousy. And he seemed to want to be friends with her. Marcia's insecurities weren't going to force Jennifer to hide somewhere, missing out on a month of fun on the island.

"Peer says we ought to try this spot," Mr. Finstad told them after slowing the boat down. "We'll do a little trolling here. The walleyes should be deep today with all this sunshine we're having."

Peer moved toward the back of the boat, then stopped near a large, metal bucket.

"What's in there?" Jennifer asked, as she watched Peer lift the hinged top of the bucket.

"The bait's in there," Marcia told her. "That's the minnow bucket."

"We're using ribbon leeches today, though," Peer said cheerfully. He pulled out a long, thin leech and held it out to Jennifer. "Put it on your hook up near its sucker end," he instructed her.

Ugh, thought Jennifer. She didn't want to take the leech, much less stick it on her hook. But if she was going to fish, she knew she was going to have to handle the bait. Gingerly, she accepted the leech from Peer.

"Better get a firm grip on it," Peer warned. "It'll stretch out when it feels that hook."

Bracing herself, Jennifer tightened her hold on the leech. Then, after locating what she decided was the sucker end, she slowly brought the leech to the hook.

Peer laughed. "Not that way," he told her.

Then, taking both her hook and the leech, he quickly slid the bait in place. "Next time, though, you're on your own." With a wink he handed her back the baited hook.

"Do mine for me, Peer," Marcia said in a wheedling voice. Without protesting or even teasing Marcia, Peer quickly baited her hook while Uncle Ben took care of his own bait.

Jennifer watched how Marcia and her uncle dropped their lines in the water, and she followed suit. Mr. Finstad slowly drove the boat backward as Peer readied a line for himself.

"This spot was hot last week on a day just like this," Peer told Uncle Ben confidently. "We'll try it for a little while, and if we don't get anything, we'll move on."

Just then, Jennifer felt a tug on her line. "Oh!" she cried, "I think I've got something!"

"Careful now," Peer advised, handing his rod to Uncle Ben and moving across the boat to sit next to Jennifer. "Let him fight but don't give him any slack. You've got to set your hook." Peer slipped his arms around Jennifer, covering her hands with his.

"Okay," he whispered against her ear. "Get ready." He tightened his grip on Jennifer's hands and helped her give her rod a mighty tug. The line made a screeching noise as it was pulled back out of her reel.

"Should I reel in?" Jennifer gasped. She could

feel Peer's warm breath on her neck. His cheek was brushing her ear. Excitement was quickly tightening all the muscles in her body.

"Not yet," he replied, and she felt his arm grow tense against hers. "The fish is fighting for its life now. You've got to let him tire himself out."

Then the screeching of the line through the reel stopped. "Now?" she asked. "Should I reel in now?"

Instead of answering, Peer began to slowly turn her hand around the reel. "Slowly," he said against her ear. "Slowly and carefully."

Jennifer had never felt so excited before. Every inch of her was tingling in anticipation. She wanted to say something to let Peer know how she was feeling, but she knew she shouldn't.

"Get the net, somebody. This is going to be a big one!" Peer announced as the fish got close enough to the side of the boat for Jennifer to see. She could tell by Peer's voice that he was as excited as she was.

As the fish finally left the water, Jennifer gasped. She hadn't been prepared for the beauty of it! It was a dark yellowish green on top with a pale greenish yellow belly. But what was truly beautiful about it was its eyes. They seemed to glow in a ghostly way.

"It can see in the dark, you know," Peer said, as if reading her mind.

She turned her head away from the fish and found herself looking right into Peer's dark eyes. He was so close that their noses were nearly touching. His arms were still around her, and for a second, Jennifer forgot there was anyone else in the boat.

"Oh," she murmured, her breath catching in her throat.

"Here's the net!" Uncle Ben cried, breaking the spell. He slipped the net under the fish, and Peer relaxed his hold on Jennifer and the rod they'd been sharing. "I'll bet it's an eight pounder!"

As Ben brought the netted fish into the boat, Peer released Jennifer.

"Look at your line," Marcia said critically. Jennifer looked at the spinning reel and saw that the line was in a hopeless tangle. "You're really lucky you didn't lose that fish. Of course, you probably would have if Peer hadn't helped you out."

Peer slipped the fish on a stringer. Then he attached the stringer to the side of the boat. "No big deal," Peer told her, taking the rod from Jennifer. "Here, you can use my rod while I untangle this. This happens a lot when the fish fights like this big guy was fighting."

"Want to try another spot?" Mr. Finstad asked.

"No way!" Uncle Ben cried. "I want to catch a fish like that! I'd save a big one like that for a trophy rather than eat it."

"I want to go in," Marcia suddenly announced.

"What's the matter?" Uncle Ben asked. He sounded both annoyed and concerned.

"I'm cold, and I've got a headache," Marcia said, petulantly. "I think I've been out on the water too much for one day."

"Maybe you're coming down with something," Uncle Ben said, sounding only concerned now. "Of course we'll go in."

When they reached the dock, Mr. Finstad suggested that they simply drop Marcia off and go back out. When Uncle Ben said he didn't want to leave her if she was sick, Marcia said, "Jennifer can stay with me."

Jennifer shrugged. "Sure, I'll stay. I don't mind. After all, I caught my fish for the day."

Uncle Ben looked relieved. "If you're sure . . ." he said hesitantly.

"I think I just need to lie down a moment, Daddy," Marcia said. "Jennifer can find a couple of aspirin for me. I'm sure I'll be just fine." She smiled meekly.

"Okay, then. But you lie down. Promise?" Uncle Ben said as he helped first Marcia and then Jennifer onto the dock.

"Here's your fish," Peer said, handing Jennifer the stringer.

"What should I do with it?" she asked.

Peer laughed. "Take it to the fish house and clean it. Or tie it up on the dock, and I'll help you clean it when we get back." Then Mr. Finstad started up the motor and the boat sped away.

"Come on," Jennifer said, turning to Marcia. "Let's go up to the cabin. Do you need any help?"

"The only help I need from you," Marcia said angrily, "is for you to stay away from Peer!"

"*What?*" Jennifer felt her fish struggling on the stringer in her hand. She knew it was struggling for air, and she felt sorry for it.

"You know what I mean. Playing helpless, allowing Peer to hold you like that. I told you he's *my* boyfriend. What kind of a creep are you, anyway? Flirting with Peer like that!" Without waiting for an answer, Marcia turned and stormed up the dock.

Jennifer thought about going after her. Then she remembered her fish. Right now, Jennifer was more concerned about the fish than her spoiled bratty cousin. *Poor fish!* she told herself, thinking of the expression "a fish out of water" that her mother liked to use. That's exactly how she was feeling. . . . Getting down on her knees on the dock, Jennifer gingerly took hold of the big fish. Then, after pulling the stringer carefully out of his mouth, she let him fall back in the water.

"You're free," she told him. Without looking back, the big, old walleye swam away.

Although Jennifer thought Marcia's jealousy

was very unreasonable—after all, she was only being friendly—for the next few days, she avoided Peer. It wasn't really very difficult. He was off most of the time working as a guide for other tourists in the nearby islands.

At the same time, Marcia seemed determined to avoid Jennifer. Jennifer was eager to stay out of her moody cousin's way, and she took every opportunity she had to go along fishing with Mr. Finstad and her uncle. But although she learned a lot about fishing from the two men, neither was much company. She needed to be around kids her own age. But Marcia never went along on the fishing trips unless Peer went too.

On days when Peer was free, he'd show up at the cabin, and Marcia would give Jennifer a withering look that said, "Don't you dare come along!" Dutifully, Jennifer would make an excuse for not going. But Peer would look at Jennifer coldly, and it was all Jennifer could do not to say anything.

When Marcia and Peer left with Uncle Ben, Jennifer would be left alone with Mrs. Finstad. Only Mrs. Finstad seemed to enjoy Jennifer's company, chatting with her while they shared the morning chores. But Mrs. Finstad was such a busy person that sometimes Jennifer had the feeling she was more of a hindrance than a help. And while she didn't mind helping around the house, she certainly hadn't planned to spend her whole vacation that way!

Everyone knew something was going on—but no one except for Jennifer and Marcia knew what. Peer and Uncle Ben seemed the most annoyed by the situation. And it seemed to Jennifer that they both blamed her, thinking her cold and unfriendly. She wished she could clear up all the misunderstandings. But she had no idea how to do that without making matters worse. After all, she had to live with Marcia.

Finally, Uncle Ben cornered Jennifer and said, "My first round of clients is arriving tomorrow, you know. Once they come, I'm going to be pretty busy entertaining them. And the boat's going to be too full for you to fish with us."

Jennifer nodded slowly. "Mrs. Finstad mentioned that your guests were coming soon."

"I don't know what to say, Jennifer," Uncle Ben confessed. "I'd hoped you and Marcia would be good company for each other. I'm afraid I don't know what's going on between you two, but it's pretty obvious that you're not getting along."

"It's all right, Uncle Ben," Jennifer assured him, hating to tattle on anyone. "I guess we're just interested in different things. It's not really that we're not getting along, you know." It wouldn't do any good to tell her uncle that she wanted to be friends with Peer, but Marcia wouldn't let her. She knew that would sound as awful to him as it sounded to her. He probably wouldn't believe her anyway.

Her uncle looked at her as if he wanted to say something else. Jennifer waited politely, but all he finally said was, "Well, I'm sure you both will be fine."

As he left, Jennifer knew he was disappointed in her. He'd invited her to come to the island so Marcia wouldn't be so alone while he worked. But instead of one lonely girl, he thought he now had two lonely girls. Jennifer felt as though she owed it to Uncle Ben to try harder to get along with her cousin. If only Marcia would realize that Jennifer wasn't after Peer. Sure, she liked him, but she wasn't interested in anything romantic with him. If only the three of them could be friends . . .

Jennifer was still thinking about the whole situation when she bumped right into someone as she was coming down the stone steps of their cabin.

"Oh!" she said, looking up to see Peer. "Excuse me. I guess I wasn't paying attention to where I was going."

"I'm the one who ought to apologize," Peer said. His dark eyes were penetrating, and Jennifer felt challenged by his gaze.

"Why?" Jennifer asked, realizing that this was

the first time she'd been face to face with him since he'd helped her land her fish.

Peer shrugged. "Why not, Jennifer? The employer's always right. If anything goes wrong, the employee's to blame no matter what actually happened."

Jennifer stared at him, confused. "I'm not your employer," she replied. "And even if I was, that's not how *I* think. Besides, I thought you were going to call me Jenny."

He said, "I don't seem to be getting a chance to call you much of anything. Every time I'm around, you run away."

Jennifer bristled at his words. She'd gone out of her way to try to please everyone, and all she was getting was grief. It was so unfair!

"That's not *my* fault," she said angrily.

"It's not!" Peer sounded genuinely surprised. "Then whose fault is it?"

Jennifer didn't know what to say. She couldn't very well accuse Marcia of keeping her away from Peer. After all, Peer was in love with Marcia. If Jennifer blamed Marcia for her behavior, it would undoubtedly make Peer even more hostile toward her, and Jennifer didn't think she could stand that on top of everything else.

"Well, I know it hasn't been my fault. I haven't been avoiding you," he said with a shrug. "Anyway, I hope you've enjoyed your fishing."

Jennifer smiled. "Yes," she told him, "and I

think you'll be glad to hear that I can now land my own fish, bait my own hook, and, thanks to your dad, even fillet my own fish."

"I'm impressed," Peer said. "Listen, I was—"

But before he could finish, he was interrupted by a voice calling, "Jennifer! Jennifer!" Jennifer turned and saw Marcia, standing in the doorway of their cabin.

"I better go see what she wants," Jennifer told Peer, annoyed that Marcia always had to interrupt her conversations with Peer.

He shrugged. Then, without saying anything else, he went on down to his own house.

Marcia was still waiting by the cabin door when Jennifer finished her climb up the steps. "What was *that* all about?" Marcia demanded, blocking Jennifer's way inside.

"What was *what* all about?" Jennifer asked wearily.

"I saw you flirting with Peer on the steps a moment ago." Marcia was wearing a tight denim mini-skirt with a long-sleeved red tee. Around her neck hung an elaborate strand of multicolored beads.

"I like your beads," Jennifer said, deliberately choosing to ignore Marcia's unreasonable accusation.

"Don't try to change the subject. What were you saying to him?" Marcia pressed. Jennifer wondered why Marcia was so insanely jealous. What kind of person did Marcia think she was?

"Well, I certainly wasn't flirting, if that's what you're worrying about. I didn't know there was a law against talking to people!"

"You weren't talking about me, were you?" Marcia asked suspiciously.

Jennifer inhaled deeply, trying her best to fight the rising urge she had to tell Marcia off. *"No!"* she finally shouted, despite her best intentions. "Not everyone is as obsessed with you as you are yourself, Marcia Brewster!" With that she pushed past her cousin and ran inside. She climbed into her loft, grabbed her journal and collapsed onto her cot. As she thumbed through her journal to find the next blank page, Jennifer heard the screen door bang shut.

Good, she told herself. She didn't care if she'd hurt Marcia's feelings. Marcia deserved it. If the tables were turned, Jennifer knew she'd be going out of her way to include Marcia in at least some of her activities with Peer. Jennifer knew she wouldn't isolate Marcia the way Marcia was isolating her.

Gazing out the cabin window, Jennifer thought about the conversation she'd just had with Peer. He definitely had the wrong idea about her motives. Here she'd gone out of her way to stay away so that he and Marcia could have time alone together. But he thought she was purposely ignoring him. What, she wondered, had Marcia said to him about her?

"Dear Kate," Jennifer wrote, her hand trembling with anger. "I'm so glad there are only three weeks left before I come home. Today . . ."

Writing her feelings down made her feel a little better. Jennifer was so engrossed in her writing that she jumped when she heard the slam of the screen door.

"Dinner," Marcia called from the bottom of the ladder. "Dad sent me to get you."

"Hi," Jennifer said, looking sheepishly down at Marcia from the loft. "Look," she added, "I'm sorry I snapped at you earlier. But this vacation hasn't been much fun for me, you know. I've gone out of my way to leave you and Peer to yourselves, since you obviously get annoyed when I even talk to Peer. I think you ought to appreciate what I've been doing. Your dad is furious with me, you know. He thinks I'm giving you the cold shoulder. Even Peer thinks I'm some sort of a snob or something. At least you could let him in on what's really happening around here. I don't appreciate people thinking I'm a jerk."

Marcia nodded, though she didn't seem very sorry. "I guess you're probably right. You have been nice about this whole mess. My father really should have asked me if I wanted you here. But that isn't your fault."

"Thanks a lot," Jennifer said sarcastically as she climbed down the ladder. "If I'd known you didn't want me here, I certainly wouldn't have come. I have better things to do. You could have written to me, you know. Anyway, I just hope your dad doesn't say something to my parents about how I'm not being friendly, or something."

"Don't worry," Marcia assured her. "Daddy isn't the type to go tattling."

"I hope not. I don't want to have to explain what's going on here to my mom. I'm not even sure *I* know what's going on here." Jennifer gave Marcia a hard look. "What is going on here, anyway?"

Marcia looked very innocent as she shrugged. "I don't know what you mean, Jennifer."

"I want to know what *you* told Peer about *me*," Jennifer said. "Does he or does he not know that *I* know about you two?"

"I guess we've been so busy getting reacquainted with each other that we haven't really gotten around to discussing you. Why? Would you like me to tell him that you know?" Marcia asked, lifting her eyebrows in an innocent looking gesture.

"Yes," Jennifer said with a conviction that startled her. "And I'd like to be able to go fishing with you two. Maybe not all of the time, but once in a while. I'm not going to be able to go

73

out with your dad once his guests arrive. It's not much fun stuck on an isolated island with no one to do things with, you know. Besides, your father would be happier if he thought you and I were getting to be friends."

Marcia sighed. "If it means so much to you, I'll talk to Peer when I get a chance and let you know what he says." Marcia got up and started toward the door. "Come on," she said over her shoulder, "Dad is waiting for us. I suppose it wouldn't do any good to get him any more upset than he already is by making him wait dinner for us."

"Marcia?" Jennifer said as she joined her cousin in the doorway.

"What?" Marcia asked.

"Talk to Peer tonight, okay? Your dad's clients are coming tomorrow sometime, and things are going to get kind of lonely for me. I'd love to go fishing with you and Peer in the morning."

Marcia pushed the screen open and stepped outside. "I'll do what I can," she said, "but I won't make any promises."

Chapter Six

The next morning, Jennifer woke up to the sun shining in her eyes. With a start, she realized she'd overslept.

After dressing quickly, she climbed down from the loft. A glance at the clock in the kitchen told her it was nearly ten. No one had even bothered to call her for breakfast! She was just about to put her own breakfast together when Mrs. Finstad popped her head in the door.

"You're up," Mrs. Finstad said, sounding surprised.

Jennifer shook her groggy head. "I guess I overslept."

Mrs. Finstad came the rest of the way into the cabin. Then she put her hand on Jennifer's forehead. "You don't feel hot," she decreed.

"Why would I?" Jennifer said, confused. "I sure am hungry though. I'm sorry I missed your great breakfast."

Mrs. Finstad laughed. "You young people are lucky. You recover so quickly."

"Recover?" Jennifer said. "Recover from what?"

"Why, Marcia told us this morning that you weren't feeling well. Mr. Brewster wanted to come over here and get you, but Marcia insisted you'd specifically asked to be allowed to sleep in. She said it was your stomach, so I thought I'd better check on you to make sure you didn't need anything."

Marcia! Jennifer told herself. *I should have known!* After their conversation the evening before, Jennifer had hoped things would get better.

"Marcia told you that, huh?" Jennifer said instead. There was no need to get Mrs. Finstad involved, Jennifer decided. Jennifer would just wait and deal with Marcia later. But deal with her, she would! Marcia had really gone too far this time.

"Well, you'd best take it easy," Mrs. Finstad said. "You might feel better now, but you never know. You don't want to have a relapse, now do you?"

"I won't be having any relapse," Jennifer assured her.

"Well," Mrs. Finstad said, "you do look fit as a fiddle. Now, I have to get back to the big cabin and make up the extra beds."

Jennifer smiled. "After I finish breakfast I'll come give you a hand. I haven't anything to do since I missed Marcia and Peer."

Jennifer gobbled down a bowl of cereal and two thick slices of delicious home baked bread. Then she headed down to the bigger cabin to help Mrs. Finstad get it ready for Uncle Ben's guests.

"How many men are coming?" Jennifer asked as they sorted a pile of sheets into sets.

"Three, this weekend. They'll eat up a storm, play cards all night, and fish all day, talking non-stop as they do." She shook her head, setting her black, silver-streaked braid in motion. "Whoever it was that said men don't gossip didn't know men the way I've come to know men."

Jennifer laughed. "What do they gossip about?" she asked.

"Other men. Oh, you should hear them going on about this one and that one!"

"Who are you talking to, Ma?" Peer asked, poking his head into the bedroom where Jennifer and his mother were working. When he saw Jennifer, he seemed surprised. "Jennifer," he said, raking his fingers through his dark hair. "I thought you were sick."

"So I've heard," Jennifer said drily. "But I'm not."

"I can vouch for that," put in Mrs. Finstad. "Thanks to Jennifer, I'm nearly done here with all my chores."

"Jennifer?" Peer said, looking surprised.

"Yes, Jennifer. You've been so busy I guess you haven't noticed what a help Jennifer's been to me."

Peer nodded. "I guess not," he confessed.

Mrs. Finstad winked at Jennifer. "Well, now you know. Where is your 'shadow,' anyway?" Mrs. Finstad teased.

Peer shrugged, his tanned cheeks turning a chestnut color. *Shadow?* Jennifer thought. Mrs. Finstad had to be talking about Marcia. And she seemed to think it was funny! The revelation stunned Jennifer.

"I don't know," Peer said gruffly, as though he were annoyed by the idea of having a 'shadow.' "I'm sure wherever Marcia is she can take care of herself just fine." Peer, it seemed, found Marcia's attention embarrassing! Jennifer realized that his feelings for Marcia weren't the same feelings she had for him. Peer hadn't been *acting* annoyed with Marcia; Peer *was* annoyed with Marcia. Marcia must have been lying all along, just to keep Jennifer away from Peer—he wasn't really Marcia's boyfriend!

"Hmmm," was all his mother said. She pursed her lips as if she were trying hard to stop herself from laughing. "That girl could use a shade more independence, if you ask me."

"I agree," Peer said. "But what can I do about it, Ma?"

Mrs. Finstad stopped smiling. "Nothing. You're handling it right, Peer. Anyway, I've got an errand that'll keep you busy this afternoon at least. I need a few things from the mainland, staples we've run low on."

"I'll take the smaller boat over for them," Peer offered. "We've finally got that old motor back in working order."

"Good," Mrs. Finstad said. "My list's on our kitchen counter by the sink. There's money in the cookie jar."

"Okay. I'll be back in a couple hours." Peer turned toward the back door.

"Wait," his mother said before he left the room. "Why don't you take Jennifer with you? She's worked enough for one day. She deserves a little outing."

"Jennifer?" Peer asked. "Want to come with me?"

Jennifer searched his handsome face to see if he really wanted her company or if he thought of her the same way he thought of Marcia, a necessary part of being the Brewsters' employee.

But his dark eyes looked inviting, and he was even smiling at her.

Smiling back, she said, "Sure, I'd like to take a trip to the mainland. In fact, I've got a couple of letters that need to be mailed."

"If you want to go get your letters, I'll meet you on the dock," Peer said, watching her finish slipping a pillow into a pillowcase. She set the pillow down, pleased by his attention. "How about five minutes?" he asked as he held the door for her.

"How about three?" Jennifer countered, pausing next to him in the doorway. She suddenly felt so free! Free to be herself—free to feel all that she knew she felt for the handsome boy next to her.

"How about last one to the dock is a rotten egg?" Peer said, tilting his head up slightly so that he was looking down his nose at her in a challenging way. Jennifer thought he seemed so tall up close like that, and so much older than sixteen.

Breaking away from his hypnotic gaze, Jennifer bolted out the door. "You're on!" she called back over her shoulder.

It felt good to be running. Jennifer felt as free as the wind. She burst into the cabin and charged up the ladder to the loft where she'd left a letter to her parents and one to Kate tucked in her journal. But when she got to her bed where she'd left her journal, the letters weren't there. Jennifer was baffled until she spotted the missing letters on the floor next to the bed. Deciding that they must have fallen out when she threw her journal on the bed, Jennifer tucked them in the breast pocket of her jean jacket.

Jennifer was about to charge out the door and down to the dock when she suddenly wondered how she looked. She hadn't thought too much about her appearance lately, Jennifer realized. Maybe her hair needed brushing, and maybe a touch of lip gloss would be a good idea. Now that she knew Peer was unattached, things like that seemed to matter a little more.

Jennifer backtracked to the bathroom and examined her reflection in the oak-rimmed mirror over the sink. Her face had gotten tan during the course of her stay on the island. She noted with pleasure that her darkened skin made her blue eyes look even bluer. Jennifer ran a brush through her long dark hair and said to her reflection, "There, that will do. I don't want to be a rotten egg."

"A what?" a voice behind her demanded. Then there was another face in the mirror next to Jennifer's. This face was also tan, emphasizing an equally dazzling pair of blue eyes. But there was no denying that even though the girls looked remarkably alike, Marcia looked better.

Jennifer looked away, feeling ashamed of the tightness in her chest that seeing Marcia had produced and of the joy she'd felt at discovering Marcia's lie about Peer.

"Oh, nothing," Jennifer mumbled. "I was just talking to myself." She wanted to push past Marcia and run down to the dock to meet Peer by herself. But she couldn't. That was something Marcia would do. Jennifer was not Marcia, nor did she want to be.

Turning to face her cousin, Jennifer said, "I'm going to the mainland with Peer to pick up some things for his mother."

"Oh?" Marcia said, raising her eyebrows. Jennifer could tell she didn't like what she was hearing.

"Want to come?" Jennifer asked, trying her best to sound as if she really wanted her cousin's company.

"Of course I'll come," Marcia said. "I'm not going to let you go with him by yourself."

Jennifer thought again of all the lies Marcia had told. Jennifer had decided that telling everyone she had been sick that morning would be the last lie of Marcia's she would tolerate. But there wasn't time to confront Marcia now. Peer was waiting.

"All right," Jennifer said, casually slipping by

Marcia. "But there's something you ought to know."

"What?" Marcia demanded.

"Last one to the dock is a rotten egg!" Jennifer yelled. With that she turned around and bolted out the door, down the steps, to the dock. Peer, she could see, was already there, waiting.

"I'm afraid you're a rotten egg," Peer said as Jennifer leaped onto the dock and dashed the last few steps to the boat.

"No, I'm not," she panted. Then she pointed at the path where Marcia was sauntering lazily in their direction. "Marcia is the rotten egg." *And that's an understatement!* Jennifer thought to herself.

"Oh, no," Peer groaned. "I suppose *she's* coming with us now."

"I had to invite her to join us," Jennifer confessed.

"Hi, there," Marcia said as she joined them alongside the boat. "I'm all set."

"Shall we tell her what she is?" Peer asked, winking at Jennifer.

Jennifer shook her head. She didn't think Marcia would enjoy the rotten egg joke. "Maybe we better just get going," she said. "You did promise your mother that we'd be back before dinner."

Peer nodded. "You're right again."

"Have you got the shopping list?" Jennifer asked.

Peer patted the breast pocket of his flannel shirt. "Right here," he replied.

Marcia flashed Jennifer a nasty look, which Jennifer returned with a smile. Marcia had tried to keep Jennifer away from Peer because she was afraid Peer liked Jennifer. *She's jealous because she knows Peer doesn't like her!* Jennifer told herself. Even though she knew Marcia deserved anything she got, Jennifer still couldn't help feeling a little sorry for her. Marcia caused herself so much trouble and pain with her negative attitude.

Once they were all in the boat, Peer pulled the cord on the outboard motor. The engine roared to life.

Peer carefully turned the boat around and slowly maneuvered them into open water. Then with a turn of his wrist, he opened the engine up, and they were off. Jennifer turned to face forward, enjoying the sensation of the spray on her face. She thought of the song that went, "The truth will set you free." Well, now she knew the truth about Peer, and she was free. The feeling was delicious!

Suddenly, Peer swerved the boat to the right of an oncoming boat. Jennifer grabbed the gunnels to keep herself from slipping off the seat. It was her Uncle Ben, returning with his clients.

Jennifer smiled and waved. She could tell by the look on Uncle Ben's face that he was very happy to see the three of them finally in the boat together.

Everyone is happy now, Jennifer thought as the smaller boat bounced over the larger boat's wake, *everyone but poor Marcia*. Jennifer had the feeling, though, that Marcia and only Marcia would be able to make herself happy.

Chapter Seven

The ride went quickly. Talking was out of the question because the roar of the motor was too loud. But Jennifer was glad for their silence. The scenery was breathtaking, and sitting up front with the spray in her face was exhilarating.

"Here we are," Peer said, cutting the engine. The boat glided to the dock, and Jennifer helped secure it to the pilings.

"I don't like the looks of that sky," Peer said as they climbed out of the boat. Jennifer followed his upward gaze and saw a patch of dark clouds festering in the distance. "Those clouds are forming fast, and they're moving this way," he added.

Marcia shook her head. "Don't be such a worry

wart," she ordered in a flirtatious way. "What's one little cloud?"

"I think we better hurry," Peer said, not responding to Marcia's teasing tone. "I don't want to get caught in a storm, especially not in this little boat." Then he said, "You have letters to mail?" Jennifer nodded. "We'll stop at the post office on our way to the grocery," he told her. Then he took the lead, moving quickly along the dock.

"For heaven's sake!" Marcia complained. She made a big show of trying to keep up. "Slow down, Peer! Not all of us have your long legs, you know."

"Do you know where the post office is?" Jennifer asked Marcia.

"Well, of course I do," Marcia said. "I know every inch of this little town."

"Peer!" Jennifer called. Peer stopped and turned around. "Marcia and I can go to the post office and meet you at the store if that would speed things up," Jennifer offered.

"I don't need to go to the post office," Marcia said. "I'll stay with Peer and you can meet *us* later."

"But I don't know where the post office is," Jennifer said. "You do."

"We'll all go," Peer said, starting to walk again. "It's right on the way to the grocery store, anyway."

After Jennifer had bought stamps at the post office for her letters and deposited them in the mailbox, the trio continued walking toward the store. The grocery store was much smaller than the supermarket Jennifer was used to at home.

On the positive side, however, shopping was quicker than it was at home. Swiftly, Peer picked the items from the shelves as his eyes traveled down his mother's shopping list. He shopped with the same intensity he had when he fished, an intensity Jennifer found exciting.

By the time the threesome came out of the grocery store, the little dark cloud that had looked so far away had not only come closer, it had also grown larger. Now nearly half the sky was an ominous charcoal gray.

"We'll just barely make it back before the storm hits if we leave right now," Peer said. He bounced the two overloaded grocery bags he'd insisted on carrying himself a little higher on his chest.

"Wait," Marcia ordered, stopping outside of the dry goods store. "I want to run in here a minute. We've come all this way. I don't want to rush right back."

"But we haven't *got* a minute this time," Peer told her. "Can't you see that? You don't want to get caught on the water in a storm, do you?"

"All I see are a few clouds," Marcia said, narrowing her blue eyes at him defiantly. "I don't get over here very often, and they're having a sale today," she added, pointing at a large sign in the window of the dry goods store. "I'm going in." With that, Marcia stuck her nose up in the air and marched into the little store.

"I'm sorry," Jennifer told Peer.

He looked surprised. "Why should *you* be sorry?"

"She is my cousin, part of my family. I don't know. I guess I feel responsible for her," Jennifer said.

Peer shook his head. "Well, you shouldn't feel responsible, and you certainly don't need to apologize. Marcia's been coming here for years, and she's always acted this way. First it was my brother Georgie that she followed everywhere. Then it was my brother Karl. Now, I guess, it's my turn."

"Poor Marcia," Jennifer said.

"You feel sorry for her?" Peer asked. Jennifer nodded. Then she looked up at the darkening sky.

"I better go in and try to hurry her along. Looks like the storm is speeding up," she said. Listening to Peer talk about Marcia made Jennifer uncomfortable. She'd been glad when she finally realized that Peer wasn't in love with Marcia. But now that Jennifer was learning more about how Peer and the rest of his family felt, she pitied her cousin even more than she had before. Marcia had to be the loneliest person Jennifer had ever met.

When Jennifer got into the dry goods store, she immediately spotted Marcia slowly working her way through a rack of flannel lined denim jackets. "We'd better get going," Jennifer told Marcia. "It's looking worse and worse outside."

"What do you think of these jackets, Jennifer?" Marcia asked, pulling the one she'd been looking at out so that Jennifer could see it better. "I mean, if they were bleached out . . . maybe a few silver studs along the pocket or something. Anyway, they're on sale."

"I don't think you need one. You have so many clothes." Jennifer said. "Come on, Marcia, you're just being silly. Let's go before the storm starts."

Marcia spun around and gave Jennifer a withering look. "*You're* being a baby. Just because Peer says it might rain, you want to rush back to the island. Well, I don't! I want to have some fun for a change. Peer doesn't know everything, you know. He puts on a good act, but he's just a boy. If his older brothers were around this summer, you'd see that."

"You're too much," Jennifer said, forgetting the pity she'd felt only minutes before. Turning away from Marcia, Jennifer stomped out of the store.

"No luck?" Peer asked when Jennifer joined

him on the sidewalk. He wearily set the grocery bags on the ground.

Shaking her head, she said, "No luck at all. Let's leave her here!"

Peer smiled. "Leave 'poor Marcia' here? Tempting," he said, "but impossible." He looked up at the sky, and Jennifer did, too. There wasn't any blue left. The entire sky was now overcast and ominous rumblings could be heard in the distance. "I suppose what we'll have to do is stay here until the storm blows over."

"But your mom needs these things," Jennifer reminded him.

"Mom would say our safety outweighed her need for butter and eggs, believe me," Peer said, picking up the groceries again.

"I guess you're right," Jennifer agreed.

"Right about what?" Marcia asked, choosing that moment to pop out of the store. Her arms were empty. Just as Jennifer had suspected, Marcia hadn't bought anything. She'd only managed to slow them down so that now they were stranded.

Jennifer turned on Marcia. "Right about the storm!" she said crossly. "Look, Marcia." Jennifer pointed at the dark sky.

Marcia shrugged. "So? Haven't you ever seen clouds before?" But before Jennifer could think of a reply, a loud clap of thunder sounded almost directly overhead. "A storm!" Marcia cried.

Peer looked at Jennifer and rolled his dark eyes. "It takes some people quite a while to catch on, wouldn't you say, Jenny?" Jennifer nodded.

"Where to now, girls?" Peer asked. "I suggest we go to the cafe for a soda and hope that this storm is a quick one."

"We've got to go back!" Marcia said, an edge of panic in her voice. "We can't stay here. There's no telling how long this storm will last. Daddy would worry."

"It's too late for that," Peer told her.

"No, it's not," Marcia insisted. Then she started down the street toward the boat.

After exchanging exasperated looks, Jennifer and Peer ran down the street to catch up with Marcia. As they neared the dock where the little motor boat was moored, Jennifer felt first one and then another drop of rain strike her face.

"We can beat this storm if we hurry," Marcia insisted. She climbed into the stern of the boat and gave the starter cord a yank.

Peer quickly handed Jennifer both bags of groceries. "Careful," he said to Marcia as he hopped into the stern of the boat. "You'll flood it, and we won't get anywhere." Then he bent over and carefully switched gas tanks so the motor would be running off the full tank. When he straightened up again, he took the groceries from Jennifer and set them on the bottom of the boat, where he wrapped them in a tarp.

"I guess we're going to make a run for it," he told Jennifer, reaching out a hand to help her aboard. As Peer's hand closed around hers, an electrical charge seemed to flow from his body to hers. *Does he feel it, too?* she asked herself hopefully. Then, as Jennifer stepped down into the cockpit, their eyes met and Jennifer knew that he had indeed felt it.

"Come on, come on!" Marcia urged frantically as another clap of thunder crashed loudly overhead. "We've got to hurry! We've got to beat the lightning!"

Peer maneuvered the boat into open water. A wind had come up, making the lake choppy and driving the rain so hard that it felt like tiny needles striking Jennifer's cheeks.

"Open it up!" Marcia ordered. Jennifer could see that Marcia was frightened. Every time thunder sounded overhead, Marcia cowered. But it was hard for Jennifer to feel much pity for her. After all, this whole mess was Marcia's fault. If she hadn't forced them to wait for her, they'd be a good twenty minutes closer to home. Jennifer told her cousin to be quiet and let Peer handle it. Marcia glared at her, but calmed down.

They were well out of sight of the mainland when a bolt of lightning flashed right above their heads, followed by a loud crash of thunder. Then, as if the lightning had broken a vast dam in the sky, the rain became a torrential downpour. Peer immediately cut the engine until they were barely crawling along.

"What are you doing?" shrieked Marcia. Jennifer could see that she was trembling.

"I can't see," Peer told her. "We're going to have to stop at the nearest island and wait this out there. If we go on, we could capsize or run into rocks. We could easily drown."

"I see something!" Jennifer cried as a dark shape materialized on the horizon in front of her.

"Thank goodness!" Peer said. "It's an island! Watch the water for rocks, Jenny. Sometimes there are big ones right below the surface."

Jennifer got on her knees and looked over the bow of the boat at the water in front of them. The lake water was very clear and usually there was no problem seeing several feet below the surface. But today, with the rain striking as hard and fast as it was, spotting submerged rocks was no easy task.

"On the right!" she cried suddenly. Peer swerved the boat just in time, and they missed the jagged rock by inches.

By now, the island was more than just a dark shape on the horizon. Jennifer could tell it was one of the smaller islands, uninhabited, but large enough to have several scruffy looking pine trees on it.

"Can you jump off on that rock ahead if I can bring us close enough to it?" Peer asked her.

Jennifer nodded. She wasn't sure whether she could or not, but she was determined to try. Getting up on the seat so that she was ready to spring, Jennifer took the rope in her right hand and concentrated on the land in front of her. The rain was still coming down by the bucketful.

"Get ready," Peer told her. Then he added, "Be careful! The rocks are going to be slippery." Jennifer braced herself and jumped.

At first Jennifer was sure she was going to fall into the water. The rock was even slipperier than it looked. She nearly let go of the rope as she clawed at the rock, trying to get a firm grip. But then, miraculously, her foot found a nitch. She felt the pull of the motor boat behind her as the waves pulled it back out. But Jennifer hung on. Then, stretching herself out as far as she could, she was able to reach the twisted trunk of a pine tree and secure the rope to it.

"Careful," Jennifer urged Marcia, holding out her hand to help her cousin out of the boat.

"I'm right behind you," Peer assured Marcia as she climbed onto the pitching bow of the boat. Marcia sprang toward Jennifer, and Jennifer grabbed her as she landed.

Peer was next. Both Marcia and Jennifer slid further up the bank of rocks to give him room.

It wasn't until all three of them were sitting safely on the island that Jennifer realized how thoroughly soaked she was. A chill ran the length of her body, and she felt herself shiver.

The boat continued to bang against the rocky wall below them. The sound of the aluminum hull clanging in protest to this rough treatment was nearly as loud as the thunder overhead. The rope appeared to be strained to the limit, and Jennifer was afraid the storm might win, taking the boat away and leaving them stranded. She shivered again.

Suddenly, she felt Peer's arm around her. "Don't worry," he said, his breath warm against her damp cheek. "We're going to be all right now that we're off the water. I'm going to get the tarp and some rope out of the boat. I'll be back in a couple of minutes."

"Be careful," she said, wishing he wouldn't leave her, afraid that he might be carried away with the boat.

"I'm always careful," he assured her, getting to his feet. His dark hair was plastered to his forehead, but his rugged jaw was set with determination.

Jennifer looked around for her cousin. "Marcia!" Jennifer called. But Marcia seemed oblivious to what was happening around her. She sat huddled on the shore, whimpering, tears mixing with the rain. Jennifer thought she looked like the loneliest person in the world. But, at least for the moment, Marcia wasn't in any real danger.

Jennifer turned her attention back to Peer and the very real danger he was facing. Peer slid down the rock to the boat, then took hold of the bow of the boat with both hands and carefully climbed back in. First, he picked up the tarp that had been protecting the groceries and stuffed it under his arm. As Jennifer continued to watch, he put a coil of rope, a First Aid kit, and several things from the bags of groceries into the pockets of his jacket.

In no time, he was safely back on the rock next to Jennifer. "I'm going to make a lean-to with the tarp to shelter us from the storm," Peer told her. "But I'm going to need help."

Peer glanced over at Marcia, who seemed practically catatonic. "Marcia!" he said sharply. But Marcia didn't move. With her arms locked around her knees, she rocked slightly back and forth, a forlorn look on her face.

"*We'll* put up the lean-to," he said in disgust, turning back to Jennifer. "We don't need Marcia's help for that. In fact, it'll probably go quicker with just the two of us."

"Will she be all right?" Jennifer whispered, glancing over at her cousin, who was staring straight ahead. As angry as she still was with Marcia, she felt sorry for her—and worried.

"The best we can do for her right now is to get that tarp up," said Peer. "I doubt if we'll be able to get a fire going. Everything is just too soaked for that. But we'll huddle close together. We should be able to keep warm enough that way—at least we'll be out of the wind and rain. I also got some food out of the boat."

Peer sounded so sure of himself, so in control of the situation, that Jennifer felt herself relax a little bit.

We're going to be all right, she told herself. *Peer's an experienced outdoorsman. He knows what to do. He won't let anything happen to us.* Jennifer decided she would just follow Peer's directions and hope that this whole nightmare would soon be over.

Chapter Eight

"Help Marcia over to that tree," Peer instructed a moment later, pointing to a sturdy pine. "We'll build the lean-to around her."

Jennifer did as she was told. Marcia was trembling and crying. "I'm sorry," she sobbed again and again. "Don't worry," Jennifer said. "Just try to relax."

After Marcia was settled again, Peer handed Jennifer a corner of the tarp. Taking the other corner himself, he tied it to the tree. When he took the corner back from Jennifer to lash it to a neighboring tree, Jennifer was surprised at the warmth of his hands. *How,* she wondered, *can Peer be so warm when I'm so cold?* She wanted to put both her hands in his and soak up some of that delicious warmth. But there wasn't time. There was work to be done, and Peer needed her help. She had to keep alert no matter how cold and tired she felt.

Once the two corners were secure, Peer used three stout sticks as stakes to secure the back of the tarp to the ground. The wind beat against the lean-to, making a harsh snapping sound. But, thanks to Peer's know-how, the tarp held.

Peer and Jennifer crawled into the lean-to, and the three of them huddled together, with Marcia sitting in the middle. Peer reached around Marcia and took Jennifer's hand. Despite the distance separating them Jennifer could feel Peer's strength travel from his hands to hers and up the length of her arms. When Jennifer shivered again, he gave her hand a comforting squeeze.

"We'll be all right now," Peer assured her, across the top of Marcia's bowed head. Jennifer searched his face and his eyes, so close yet so far away from her. Once again, Marcia was separating them. *Does he feel what I feel?* she asked herself.

Marcia moaned slightly. "Marcia!" Jennifer cried, letting go of Peer to give her cousin a fierce hug, "It's okay, stop crying."

Jennifer felt a genuine tenderness for her forlorn looking cousin, even though it *was* her fault they'd gotten into this mess. Jennifer was afraid Marcia might go into shock.

"Peer!" Marcia murmured. "Oh, Peer, I'm sorry. This is all my fault." She collapsed into his arms.

"It's okay," Peer, said, stroking her head, trying to comfort her. "We're okay and so's the boat. As soon as the rain lets up, we'll head home."

"Please hold me," Marcia whispered, nestling closer to Peer. "I'm so scared."

Watching Peer hug Marcia, Jennifer felt an uncomfortable and unfamiliar twinge grip her stomach. She suddenly realized that she was jealous. It wasn't a revelation that Jennifer was particularly proud of, especially after having been so worried about Marcia only seconds earlier.

Ashamed of her reaction, Jennifer felt herself tense. Looking up, she realized that Peer had seen her reaction and had understood it. Taking his arms quickly away from around Marcia, he began rummaging in the pockets of his soggy jean jacket.

"It isn't much," he said, handing each girl an apple and a chocolate bar. "But it's something. I didn't have a lot of time to think about what to take out of the boat."

Jennifer smiled. "This looks wonderful," she assured him.

"Are you okay now, Marcia?" Jennifer asked. Her cousin seemed withdrawn and sad.

Peer put one arm around Marcia again. "Marcia?" he said, "Eat your apple and your chocolate."

Marcia seemed to perk up a bit. She smiled a little at Peer.

"I think it's important that we eat. It'll help us stay warm," said Peer.

Marcia sidled up to Peer. "You'll keep me warm, won't you?" she said as she laid her head against his broad shoulder.

Jennifer had to grit her teeth to control her anger. It seemed as if Marcia was flirting and even though Jennifer knew that Peer wasn't flirting back, she didn't like it. She didn't like feeling jealous either. But she couldn't stop herself.

Peer put both his arms around Marcia again. "We'll all do our best to keep each other warm. From the sound of the thunder, the storm is moving away from us. Now all we really have to worry about is getting home again before dark." They sat together silently for a while. Marcia drifted off to sleep in Peer's arms.

Jennifer crunched into her apple, then took a bite of chocolate. She was concentrating on being warm when suddenly she found herself looking right into Peer's eyes. He carefully freed one of his arms from around Marcia, then, and reached for Jennifer's hand. She held her apple up to his lips, and he took a bite. Then Jennifer took another bite herself. She offered Peer the next one, and then each took another until all that was left was the core.

Peer smiled contentedly. "Thank you," he said.

Marcia slowly woke up. She nestled into Peer's shoulder for a moment, then lifted her head and looked at Jennifer as if she'd just become aware that she and Peer weren't alone. "Jennifer?" she said.

Jennifer forced herself to smile. "Feeling better?" she asked.

"The rain's letting up," Peer announced before Marcia could answer. He let go of both girls and got down on all fours to look around the corner of the tarp. "The wind's died down some, too. Cozy as this is, girls, I think we'd better pack it up and head for home. It's got to be getting late."

Peer crawled out of the lean-to first and stood up. "Blue sky!" he announced. "But it's tinged with pink. I'm afraid the sun's starting to go down. We've got to hustle!"

Jennifer and Marcia crawled out. This time Marcia was able to help. She and Jennifer took the tarp down while Peer did his best to scoop out some of the rainwater that had collected in the boat. Then the girls gathered the groceries that had spilled out of the ruined paper bags and put them into the tarp.

By the time they were ready to shove off, both the rain and the wind had stopped completely. The clouds were now fluffy balls of cotton tinged with brilliant oranges, pinks, and purples instead of the ominous black dome they had been before. The lake was like glass, reflecting the showy sunset above.

Automatically, they each took up their positions in the boat. Peer, the pilot, sat in the stern with the motor. Marcia sat in the middle, holding the tarp together so the groceries wouldn't spill again. Jennifer performed the duty of untying the boat, then leaped from the rock to her seat in the bow.

As the boat cut through the water, bringing them closer and closer to the Brewsters' island, a wave of sadness swept over Jennifer. She finally knew what it was like to feel jealous.

Before, with Mark, she'd thought she never felt jealous because she wasn't the kind of girl who got jealous. Now, she knew the truth. She'd never gotten jealous because she'd never cared about Mark the way she cared about Peer! Still, she didn't like the feeling.

But did Peer care for Jennifer the way she was now sure she cared for him? Or was Jennifer just as foolish as her cousin?

As Peer cut the engine to land the boat, Jennifer's head was swimming with questions, questions that only Peer could answer.

"Here they come!" Jennifer heard Mrs. Finstad yell. The woman was running down the dock toward them. "Thank goodness you're all right, all of you."

Jennifer handed Peer's mother the line just as Uncle Ben and George Finstad clattered onto the dock. Then all three of them were being whisked off, Peer with his parents and Jennifer and Marcia with Marcia's father.

"I knew Peer would handle things," Uncle Ben said, as he herded the girls into their cabin. "But we were still worried."

"You should have seen him, Daddy," Marcia said. "He was wonderful. He built us a shelter from the wind and got us food and—"

"I'm sure he did just fine," Uncle Ben said. "But you can tell me all about it later. Now you girls need to shower and get into dry clothes."

Jennifer did feel exhausted. Unable to stand any longer, she collapsed onto the nearest chair.

Uncle Ben said, "I'm going to go back now and tell the others that you kids are safe and sound. All the men were as worried as I was. Anyway, Darlene will be up shortly with some dinner for you."

As soon as her father had left, Marcia surprised Jennifer by saying, "You can take the first shower. I'll just get out of my wet clothes and slip into my robe and slippers. I can wait."

"Thanks," Jennifer told her gratefully. "If you're sure it's okay."

"I'm sure. Really, I am," Marcia insisted.

Jennifer was too tired to argue. Besides, at the moment, a hot shower was just what she needed to revive.

As she stood under the soothing spray, she reflected on the day. So much had happened that Jennifer was having trouble sorting it all out.

Stepping out of the shower into the steamy bathroom, Jennifer rubbed her skin pink with a soft fluffy towel. Then she slipped into her plaid flannel nightgown and her heavy terry cloth robe. She hadn't brought any slippers with her, so she had to settle for a clean pair of woolen socks. Finally, she wrapped her wet hair turban-style in a dry towel.

"The bathroom's all yours," she called to Marcia.

"I'm in the living room," Marcia called back cheerfully.

Jennifer walked through the bedroom to the living room. There she found Marcia, dressed in a pink satin robe and matching slippers, curled on the couch, looking very much like the cat that had gotten not just one canary but the entire flock.

"Thanks for letting me go—" Jennifer began. But before she could get it all out, she spotted Peer. He was sitting on the floor busily building a fire.

"Peer's here," Marcia said, stating the obvious.

"Hi!" Peer said, looking up at Jennifer from his place on the floor. He smiled, startling Jennifer into remembering that not only was her hair a tangled mess but she was also dressed in flannel and terry cloth. She knew that in comparison to the way Marcia was dressed, she had to look shabby, and not very appealing.

"Um . . . hi," Jennifer said self-consciously, staring down at the wool socks on her feet.

"Hi," Peer said again. Then he added, "Well, that should do it." Peer got to his feet. "Either one of you can do the rest. The matches are on the mantel in the tall box. Dad wanted to do this, but I had to make sure myself that you were both all right."

"Don't run out now," Marcia said, sticking her lower lip out in a mock pout.

Peer said, "I've got an early job tomorrow. Your dad asked me to be the guide for his group. I don't want to be so tired that I blow that kind of opportunity."

Marcia sighed dramatically. "No, you don't want to do that."

Peer paused by the couch to rumple Marcia's hair, and Jennifer felt herself gasp involuntarily. Had Peer changed his mind? Did he like Marcia after all?

But before Jennifer could figure out exactly what was going on, Peer had crossed the room and was standing in front of her. "You look much better, Jenny," he said, focusing his dark eyes on her.

"I do?" Jennifer said, thinking of her tangled

hair and terry robe. She felt like turning and fleeing to the sanctuary of the bathroom, but she was simply too embarrassed to move.

Then she felt Peer's warm fingers gently grazing her cheek. He stepped closer to her, his face as close as it could be without actually touching hers.

"Really," he said, "you do. I was worried about you, you know." Then he slowly traced the outline of her lips with his finger. "Mom sent a casserole up. I put it in the oven. I'd like to stay, and help you enjoy it and that fire you're going to have. But I can't."

"I understand," Jennifer managed to say as she walked him to the door. *He likes me!* she told herself joyfully. *And he's not afraid to let Marcia see that he does, either.*

"But I'll see you soon," he promised. He gave her shoulders a squeeze and leaned forward. Suddenly his lips met hers in a warm, tender kiss. Peer gazed solemnly into her eyes for a moment, then gave her a hug and was gone.

Jennifer sighed, and stood motionless as the cabin door shut.

"You look ridiculous," Marcia snapped in her ear. Somehow her cousin had crossed the room without Jennifer's noticing. Then Marcia went into the bathroom, slamming the door shut.

Once she was alone, Jennifer crossed the room to the couch and settled into the spot where

Marcia had been sitting. The fabric was still warm—just as Peer's lips had been. . . . She began to towel-dry her hair.

Am I being a fool by allowing myself to be attracted to Peer? she asked herself. Jennifer thought about Peer's dark eyes, his broad shoulders, his warm, strong hands. "Peer," she whispered, wishing he was there beside her. She couldn't deny how she felt about him. But would she ever know how Peer really felt about her? True, he had kissed her. But although he claimed not to like Marcia, Jennifer couldn't help remembering how tender he had been toward Marcia during the storm. And there was no denying the fact Marcia was the prettier and more fashionable of the two girls.

And getting involved with Peer was risky since Jennifer only had a few more weeks on the island. Although Jennifer couldn't deny her feelings for him, she decided that she should try to keep things casual with Peer. It would be easier all around that way.

By the time Marcia finally came out of the shower, Jennifer had the table all set for dinner. She'd started the fire with the matches Peer had left for them. A warm glow blanketed the rooms.

"Are you hungry?" she asked Marcia.

Marcia shrugged. "I guess so," she said moodily.

As the girls ate dinner Jennifer tried to carry on a friendly conversation. But despite the fact that she did her best to avoid the subject of Peer, Marcia kept bringing him up. "You saw how Peer took care of *me* today," Marcia said, gloating. "He just kissed you because he felt sorry for you. You don't have a chance with Peer no matter what you might think." Marcia looked so smug and sure of herself that Jennifer once again wondered what Peer's brief kiss had meant. "So there's no use chasing after him—you'll only embarrass yourself."

Jennifer took a deep breath to control her temper. "I have no intention of *chasing* after anyone. I'd like for us to be friends. We'll only be here a couple more weeks. Can't we *try* to get to know each other and have a little fun? What do you say?"

Marcia didn't say anything. Instead, she got up and went to her room, leaving Jennifer to face another lonely night on her own.

Chapter Nine

When the sky turned pink with the dawn, Jennifer was glad that she could finally get out of bed. She had tossed and turned all night. Try as she might, she just hadn't been able to put thoughts of Peer out of her mind. And she was no closer to a solution to her problem with Marcia than she'd been before.

Jennifer dressed quietly, glad that Marcia was still asleep. A quiet breakfast, she hoped, would clear her head and help her decide what to do. She had to figure out how to avoid being alone with Peer again.

It certainly wasn't a day for moping. The sun was quite warm, already, and the sky was a deep blue. Jennifer was sprinkling sugar on her cornflakes, scribbling her thoughts about

111

Peer down in her journal, when there was a knock on the door.

"Come in!" she called. She turned around, expecting to see Mrs. Finstad or her uncle. Instead, she saw Peer. He was standing in the doorway, giving her a mischievous smile. Her breath caught in her throat as she searched his face.

"Hi," he said cheerfully. Peer didn't seem to be embarrassed about the kiss he'd given her the night before. In fact, he looked quite relaxed.

Jennifer closed her journal and got up from the table. "Marcia's sleeping. Let's go outside so we don't wake her." She left her journal and the dishes on the table and followed Peer outside. Her heart was thumping wildly at seeing him again so soon.

"You look relieved to be outside," Peer teased, once they were out the door. "What do you write in that journal anyway?"

Jennifer blushed. "Most of it's just about the way this island looks, and hiking and fishing and stuff like that. But some of it is about . . . well . . . It's all pretty confusing, actually," she stammered.

"Am *I* in it?" he asked, tilting his head slightly and giving her a sideways glance. He looked so adorable that Jennifer wanted to forget all about her decision and throw her arms around his neck.

"Maybe," she teased instead.

112

Peer smiled. "Sounds pretty interesting. Maybe I should sneak a peek at it sometime."

"No way!" Jennifer blushed again, thinking about all the things she had said about him—some good, some bad, but all terribly embarrassing.

"Don't worry, I'd never read it without your permission. That's your private stuff," Peer reassured her. "Anyway, the real reason I came by was to ask if you'd like to go swimming with me. It's so warm today, and we could take your uncle's boat since he won't be going out fishing today. I thought it would be fun to spend some time together."

"I'd like to go swimming . . ." Jennifer began cautiously.

"But?" Peer supplied, leaning against a tree.

"Excuse me?"

"You were about to say, 'I'd like to go swimming, but—' But what?"

"No buts," Jennifer said. "It's just that I'm sure Marcia would like to go, too."

"Marcia!" Peer shouted. "What do you want her along for? She always ruins everything."

"Shhh," Jennifer told him, pressing her fingers to her lips. "She's still asleep." Jennifer gestured toward the open bedroom window overhead.

"If she's sleeping, how is she going to go swimming with us?" Peer demanded. "Look, we could go out now while she's still sleeping and be back before she even knows we went." He looked at Jennifer with sudden longing. "I'd really like some time alone to talk. But maybe you don't want to be alone with me. I mean, after what happened yesterday . . ." Peer let his voice trail off as if he wasn't quite sure what had or hadn't happened the day before. "So anyway, what do you say?"

"I do want to go swimming. I'm sure there are some great spots to swim around here. I haven't been out much—except for yesterday—here, and I was beginning to feel restless," Jennifer told him, eager to avoid a discussion of the night before. "But I know that Marcia would be terribly disappointed if we went without her."

"After the stunt she pulled yesterday, I'd think you'd be glad to go without her," Peer said. "Getting stuck in that storm wasn't exactly my idea of fun, and it could have been avoided."

"Shh!" Jennifer said again, flashing Peer a warning look. "She'll hear you! Marcia may have done some silly things in the past, but she's my cousin, and I'm her guest and besides, I finally think I'm beginning to understand her. She's so lonely."

Peer shrugged. "Oh, all right then. If that's what you want, go ahead and ask her. I'll be down on the dock waiting."

"Peer," Jennifer called after him as he started to leave.

114

He turned back. "What?" he asked.

"Thanks," she said. "I just know this is going to mean a lot to Marcia."

"Sure," he said half-heartedly. "I'll see you both in a little bit then."

"Make it a half-hour," pleaded Jennifer.

"All right," Peer agreed. With that, he left.

Jennifer went back inside and sat down to eat breakfast. As she helped herself to a quick glass of orange juice she thought about kissing Peer again. *What will I tell Kate about this?* Jennifer wondered. *It doesn't even make sense to me. I really owe it to her to say something about it in my journal, though.*

Jennifer went to get her journal. She'd left it on the table with her book when she and Peer had gone outside to talk. It was gone! Jennifer looked all over the kitchen, under the table, on the chairs, but her journal was nowhere to be found. *Oh no!* Jennifer thought, *Marcia must have taken it!*

Just then Marcia's bedroom door opened. "I thought you were still asleep," Jennifer said, sitting down in a chair. "Your door was closed and . . ." She let her voice trail off as she realized that Marcia had been crying.

"Hey," Jennifer said, "what's wrong?" Jennifer was afraid she already knew the answer to her question.

"Why?" Marcia snapped. "What do you care? It's not as if we're friends, is it?"

"I thought that—" Jennifer began.

But Marcia cut her off. "You do a lot of thinking, don't you? And you don't keep many of those thoughts to yourself, either, do you? Let me see if I can remember it right. 'Marcia is an arrogant, selfish, spoiled brat. If one more person tells me how much we look alike, I think I'll scream!' I may have misquoted a word or two, but I think I got the general tone right. Don't you, *cousin*?"

Jennifer drew back in horror. "You read my journal!" she cried. "How dare you go through my private things."

"You *wanted* me to read it. Otherwise you wouldn't have left it lying around the way you did. 'Dear Kate,' you write before everything, but you might as well have addressed those entries directly to me! You wanted to hurt my feelings, but you were too afraid to do it to my face. So you wrote it down, hoping I'd read it. Well, I did."

"Then you know everything," Jennifer said. She felt as if the wind had been knocked out of her.

"About your feelings for Peer, you mean? Yes, I know that, too."

Jennifer shook her head. "I don't know what to say, Marcia. I really didn't mean to hurt you, but I must say you had it coming, snooping around in my stuff. And being here on vacation with you hasn't been any picnic either, you know. I wrote those things because you hurt me and I was lonely."

"Lonely," said Marcia sarcastically. "What do *you* know about being lonely? I've spent most of my life alone. I'm never in one place long enough to make any friends. My mother never wanted me in the first place and my father doesn't know what to do with me. I'm just a nuisance to them both." Marcia was really crying hard at that point.

"I'm sorry," Jennifer said. She felt terrible. "But you know, you don't make it very easy for people to be friendly to you."

"You have a real home—with a mother and father and you all live together, all the time," Marcia continued as if she hadn't heard. "You have friends like Kate, and a boyfriend. I had to make up a boyfriend. And then when there was the tiniest chance that Peer had actually begun to notice I'm alive, you had to butt in." Marcia glared at Jennifer.

Jennifer felt herself blush at the thought of Peer's kiss. Trying to keep her voice level she said, "I don't know what you mean. Peer likes you. I know he does. Look at the way he took care of you when we were marooned on that island."

"Maybe you're right," Marcia said, trying to stop sobbing. "Or maybe he just feels that I'm one of his duties, you know, like you wrote in your journal."

"I was wrong," Jennifer said, feeling bad that her cousin had such an empty life. "Peer likes you a lot. I think he likes us *both*, for that matter. He may not be madly in love with either one of us, but isn't it better that way? You and I will only be here another couple of weeks anyway. I think it's about time the three of us started having some *fun* together. Don't you?"

"I-I'd like that," Marcia said, sniffing slightly.

"I would too. You're the only friend here I've got."

"You'll have to forgive me for something, though," Marcia said, looking worried. "It's about your journal. I'm sorry, I was so upset . . . I tore it up, Jennifer, and threw it on your cot in the loft."

Jennifer felt angry all over again. Just when she'd thought she finally understood her cousin, Marcia had to drop another bomb.

"How could you?" she said in a low voice.

"I'm sorry. I was reading something over again, the part about the time you caught the fish and Peer's arms were around you. . . ." Marcia started to cry again.

"Peer!" cried Jennifer. "Oh, my gosh! I forgot all about going swimming!"

"What do you mean?" Marcia asked.

"Peer was here earlier. I thought you were

asleep. Anyway, he said your dad wasn't using the boat this morning—"

Marcia broke in to say, "He's too busy *packing* to go out fishing. He's going off with his clients for a few days. They're leaving in a couple hours."

"Oh. Well, Peer just said he'd take us out swimming somewhere," Jennifer went on. "He's waiting on the dock for us. Or, at least he was."

"For both of us?" Marcia asked. She sounded so pleased that Jennifer knew she'd done the right thing to insist Marcia come along. Maybe Peer did like Jennifer as much as she liked him, but in a couple of weeks Jennifer would be gone. Peer would forget all about her. Jennifer couldn't hurt Marcia by pairing up with Peer—although she knew Marcia would have done just that if given the chance. *Maybe I'm too naive,* Jennifer thought, *but I can't go out of my way to hurt people.* Jennifer glanced over her shoulder at the clock in the kitchen. "Darn!" she said. "It's even later than I thought!"

"Run down to the dock and tell him to wait for us. We'll have to change into our swimsuits." Marcia ordered. Then, apparently realizing how bossy she sounded, she added, "I want to rinse my eyes, too, so they don't look so red." She gave Jennifer a tentative smile.

"Okay," Jennifer agreed. Then she turned and dashed out of the cabin, down the rocky steps to the dock. But before she'd taken even one step onto the dock, Jennifer saw that the fishing boat was gone, and there was no sign of Peer!

Slowly, Jennifer climbed back up the stairs to the cabin. *What was Peer thinking?* she wondered. Much as she wished she hadn't, Jennifer knew she'd returned his kiss the day before. That had undoubtedly told Peer how she felt about him—something she now wished he didn't know.

Jennifer and Marcia had just begun the first shaky steps to friendship. The three of them having a good time together would undoubtedly cement that bond and perhaps give Marcia a bridge to other friendships. Jennifer wanted to be able to do that for her cousin.

"I'm back," Jennifer said dully as she pulled the cabin door open.

"Where's Peer?" Marcia asked. Her make-up looked fresh, and she'd changed her top to a bright blue and white striped tunic.

Jennifer shrugged. "He's gone," she answered.

"Where?" Marcia demanded, sounding more like her old self.

"I don't know where, but somewhere in the boat. My guess is that he got tired of waiting for us and went out alone."

Marcia looked angry, and Jennifer braced herself for the blame she suspected Marcia was about to lay on her. But Marcia only sighed. "I knew this was too good to be true," she said.

"All's not lost, you know," Jennifer assured her. "I mean, he will be back. We'll explain that we got to talking and didn't pay attention to the time. Meanwhile, let's talk. I'm dying to hear about your school in Switzerland."

"You are?" Marcia said. She sounded surprised.

"Sure. Granted, there are nice parts to living in the same place all your life, but it's not exactly glamorous or exciting. Come on. I'll make some cocoa. My mom always says there's nothing like a cup of hot cocoa after a good cry. Sound good?" asked Jennifer.

Marcia nodded. "You know, it really does sound good. I've always wanted to learn how to make cocoa."

"You have?" said Jennifer as the girls walked to the stove together.

"Well," Marcia confessed with a giggle, "I've always wanted to learn to cook, and it's a start, right?"

Jennifer couldn't help giggling herself. Maybe things would be all right after all.

Chapter Ten

"I guess I'll go back to my father's cabin and say goodbye," Marcia told Jennifer as they put their cocoa mugs away.

Jennifer said, "I'll come with you."

"No," Marcia said. "I better go alone. I haven't been very pleasant to him lately. In fact, I've been pretty nasty. I want to apologize."

"All *right*!" Jennifer cried, giving her cousin a quick hug. "That's a great idea. I'm sure your dad will appreciate that. I'd like to say goodbye, too, but my goodbye can wait until later."

"I won't be long," Marcia told her. "We can go swimming when I come back if you want. Maybe Peer will even be back then. We can see if he wants to go swimming with us."

"It's a deal," Jennifer said.

After Marcia was gone, Jennifer climbed up to her loft. She had just started putting her journal back together when she heard the cabin door slam shut. "Back so soon?" she called down from the loft, assuming it was Marcia.

"What happened to you?" It wasn't Marcia. It was Peer, and his voice sounded accusing. "I waited for you at the dock."

Jennifer started down the ladder. "I'm sorry. It took awhile to get out of here. By the time we got to the dock you were gone."

"I thought you weren't coming," Peer told her.

"You could have waited a little longer . . . I said we'd come meet you," Jennifer said, surprised at the angry tone of her own voice.

"Since you didn't show, I decided I'd go fishing. If I'd waited any longer I'd have missed the fish," Peer said sulkily. "They're the only thing I can count on around here."

"What do you mean?" Jennifer asked.

But Peer didn't answer her question. Instead, he only shrugged.

"Listen," Jennifer said hastily, "I'm really sorry we didn't make it to the dock earlier but . . . Marcia found my journal and read it—she was pretty upset at some of the things I'd written."

"What a jerk!" Peer said. "She deserved to be upset." Peer looked down at his hands for a moment, then he looked up at Jennifer. There was a challenge in his eyes.

Jennifer smiled. "I know. But Marcia really isn't as bad as she seems. I mean, I misjudged her myself. She hasn't exactly had an easy life."

Peer's eyebrows flew up at that. "She hasn't? She not only has everything she needs, she gets everything she wants."

"Everything but a mother and father who have room for her in their busy lives. She's the saddest, loneliest person I know," said Jennifer.

"Well, since Marcia's not here, you'll come have an afternoon picnic with me *alone*—right?"

Jennifer shook her head. "You don't understand. Marcia needs my friendship. She needs your friendship, too. Peer, I *really* like you. I'd love to spend the rest of the month with you— but I can't. It would kill Marcia and I won't hurt her like that." Jennifer was crying now. She had to make Peer understand. She didn't want to hurt him any more than she wanted to hurt Marcia.

Peer's dark eyes searched Jennifer's teary blue ones. He looked confused, and a little hurt, but it was obvious that he really cared about Jennifer.

"I'm sorry Peer," whispered Jennifer. "But Marcia's father is just abandoning her here to go off with his friends. She could really use some cheering up."

"All right," Peer said, taking Jenny's hand gently in his own. "I wanted to take you to a special island for a picnic—alone—but if it means that much to you, we can all go. I'll go clean the fish and meet you at the dock in, say, half an hour. And this time," he added with a smile, "don't stand me up." Peer reached up and wiped a tear from Jennifer's cheek, then turned and walked slowly out of the cabin.

Jennifer sighed and sank into a chair. She felt responsible for everyone. But everyone wanted something different, and it didn't seem possible for anyone to have what he or she wanted.

"I'm back," Marcia called cheerfully a little while later, swinging into the cabin. "Ready for that swim? If we get our suits on right now, we can get down to the dock in time to wave good-bye to Daddy."

"Peer was here," Jennifer said, wiping the last of her tears on her shirt sleeve.

"He was?" Marcia said, sounding surprised. "Did he say why he didn't wait for us this morning?"

"When we didn't come down to the dock right away, he figured we weren't coming at all. He decided to go fishing."

"That doesn't surprise me."

"Well, he invited us to have a picnic with him. He's gone to clean the fish and says we should meet him on the dock in . . ." Jennifer paused to look at her watch. "Oh, no! We're supposed to meet him in *two* minutes! If we're late again, he's going to be really mad."

"Come on then," Marcia said. "I'm all set. How about you?"

Briefly, Jennifer considered brushing her hair or changing her jeans . . . but what was the use of that? Peer had seen her at her worst and didn't seem to notice. And it would be worse to be late. "Sure," she told Marcia. "I'm all set, too."

When the girls got down to the dock, they found lots of commotion. Uncle Ben and his guests were loading the big speed boat with Peer and Mr. Finstad's help. Peer, Jennifer saw, had already stashed a picnic hamper in the smaller motor boat.

"Goodbye, Uncle Ben," Jennifer told her uncle, giving him a quick kiss on the cheek. "Have a good trip."

Uncle Ben chuckled. "You girls," he said shaking his head. "You both sound as if I was going away for good and leaving you alone on a deserted island or something. The Finstads will take good care of you both, and I'll be back in a few days."

"We know, Daddy," Marcia said, sounding a bit aloof. It was obvious she resented her father's leaving. "We'll be *just* fine."

"Of course we will," Jennifer agreed. "It's just that we're going to miss you," she added.

As if following her cousin's lead, Marcia said, "That's right, Daddy. We're going to miss you."

"I haven't spent much time with you girls, have I?" Uncle Ben said, straightening up and looking from Marcia to Jennifer and back again. He shook his head. "No, I haven't. But when I get back, I will. We'll go fishing. We'll do some exploring in the speed boat, too. There are lots of interesting things to see around here."

"Come on, Ben. We'll miss our connection if we don't get going," one of the other men said impatiently.

"Well, be good, girls. I'll see you in a couple of days." Then Uncle Ben hopped into the boat with the others and they sped away.

"You know," Marcia said to Jennifer as they watched the boat grow smaller, "I don't feel nearly as bad as I thought I would. I guess it's all thanks to you—and Peer. I've really got friends to be with for a change."

Jennifer nodded. Then she stole a quick look at Peer who was busily loading gas onto the boat. "That's good," she said absently. Pretending all she felt for Peer was friendship was going to be one of the hardest things Jennifer had ever done. Just the sight of his muscular arms and large, capable hands took her breath away. Jennifer knew there had to be a way to work all this out.

Peer looked up and caught Jennifer staring at him. Their eyes locked. He smiled, then winked. "Come on," he said, continuing to look into Jennifer's eyes. "Everything's all ready." For a second Jennifer wished that Marcia would disappear so that she and Peer could be alone for the afternoon.

"It's really nice of you to take us out like this," Marcia said to Peer. He turned to look in Jennifer's direction, raising his eyebrows comically. Marcia was actually being nice, Jennifer noticed, not coy and possessive, just plain friendly. Maybe this picnic would be fun after all, she thought.

The sun was hidden behind clouds, and there was a mild breeze, but it was nothing formidable. The little motor boat sliced easily through the choppy surf, occasionally spraying Jennifer. The sun was warm, though, and the water felt cool and refreshing on her face.

Once they were out of sight of the island, Jennifer was lost. Out on open water everything looked the same to her. Turning slightly in her seat, she watched Peer with admiration. He was able to cruise these waters so confidently, always knowing exactly where he was. His concentration was amazing. The wind blew his dark hair away from his face, revealing his surprisingly high forehead and the square cut of his lean jaw. *Why,* Jennifer asked herself, *does he have to be so handsome?* She groaned inwardly and tried to think of something else. But the memory of his kiss kept creeping into her mind.

"Here we are!" Peer finally said after cutting the engines.

"This place looks familiar," Marcia said slowly, her eyes scanning the rocky shoreline.

"That's because we've all been here before." Peer smiled mysteriously.

Getting on her toes on the bow seat, Jennifer prepared to jump to the rocks with the rope. As soon as she sprang, she knew where they were. Turning around, she said, "This is the island we landed on during the storm, isn't it?"

Peer nodded. "I thought we should come back here. It's really a great place when it's not storming."

"How can you say that?" Marcia demanded. "It's a horrible place! We could have all been killed in that terrible storm."

"We weren't, though, were we? Anyway, something happened that day that I don't think I'm ever going to forget," Peer said, fixing his dark eyes on Jennifer.

"Jennifer!" Marcia called. "Tie us up! If this is where we're actually going to stay, I want to get out of the boat." Marcia sounded like her old bossy self, giving orders, thinking of herself first.

"This is where we're staying," Peer assured Marcia as he shut the engine off. Then he pulled the motor up, out of the water.

Jennifer wrapped the rope around the same scrubby pine she'd used the day of the storm. *Please, Marcia*, thought Jennifer, *don't spoil this day*. Jennifer knew she was crazy to think that Marcia would change radically overnight, but she still had high hopes that the picnic wouldn't be a total disaster.

"Let me get out first," Jennifer heard Peer say to Marcia. "Then I can help you out."

"I can get out on my own just fine, thank you," Marcia huffed, blocking Peer's way to the bow of the boat. "Jennifer managed to get out without your help, didn't she?" Marcia added.

"Here," Jennifer said, scrambling back down the rock. "Give me your hand, Marcia. I'll help you."

"What *is* this?" Marcia demanded. "A conspiracy or something? You're both treating me like I'm a cripple."

"We're just trying to help," Jennifer said.

"The biggest help you can give me is to get out of my way, both of you!" With that, Marcia stepped onto the bow seat and promptly fell overboard.

Jennifer braced herself on the rocks and reached a hand out to grab Marcia. "Are you okay?" she asked as her cousin surfaced.

"I'm fine and I don't need your help," Marcia insisted. But the rock proved too slippery at its base for Marcia to manage climbing out without help. Finally, she accepted Jennifer's hand.

"Great," Peer said exasperated. "With that stiff breeze, we have to head right back, or you'll get a chill." He glared at Marcia. "Luckily, there's a blanket in the stern." Peer flung the blanket at Marcia who stood dripping on the shore.

"So," Jennifer said, forcing herself to sound cheerful despite the obvious tension between all three of them. "What's the big deal anyway? We'll go back and have a shore lunch right on our own island."

"That's right," Marcia said. "You got to do what you came for. We might as well go." She reached out and pulled the boat closer to the rock.

"What are you talking about?" Peer said, reaching his hand out to help Marcia aboard. "We came for lunch and none of us have eaten a thing."

Marcia pushed Peer's hand away. "I don't need *your* help! And you know full well that you didn't come here for any lunch. You came to let me know what you think of me, didn't you? You

131

came here to rub it in, to remind me that getting caught in the storm was all *my* fault! You came here to make me look foolish. Well look at me!" she yelled, holding out her dripping arms. "Do I look foolish enough now or do you want me to fall in the water again?"

"Come on, Marcia," Jennifer said. "No one made you fall in."

Marcia stumbled clumsily into the boat. "I'm not dumb. I know when I'm being punished."

"Don't be silly," Jennifer said, climbing in after her.

"Don't worry," Marcia said as Jennifer sat down. "I'm through being silly. It was silly to think we could actually be friends, to think that the three of us could have a good time together. Well, I don't think those things anymore." Marcia pulled the blanket tight around herself. An uneasy silence settled over the boat. "Go," Marcia ordered, "before I catch pneumonia."

With that, Peer started the motor and they were speeding back to the island. Jennifer was too depressed to even cry. She reminded herself that in two weeks it would all be over. But somehow knowing that didn't help much—two weeks sounded like an eternity.

When they got back to the island, Jennifer caught the dock and tied up the boat. Peer hopped out and offered his hand to Marcia. She refused, preferring instead to stumble out on her own. Then she ran off in the direction of the cabin. Jennifer was sure she was crying again.

Then Peer turned his attention to Jennifer. She took his hand and let him pull her to the dock. "Let her go," Peer said, still holding Jennifer's hand. He pulled her closer toward him.

"No," Jennifer said, struggling to free herself from the mesmerizing effect of his touch. "She needs me."

"I need you too," said Peer, his eyes flashing. Jennifer looked away.

"Come on, Jennifer. That's the way Marcia has always acted when things don't go according to her plans," Peer insisted, tightening his grip on Jennifer so that his fingers were almost hurting her.

"You're wrong," Jennifer insisted. "Marcia can be nice. I know she can. Just this morning—"

Peer didn't let her finish. He withdrew his hand and backed away from her. "Fine," he said stiffly. "Go after her. It's obvious that all you care about is Marcia. I'm through trying to stop you. Maybe I am wrong about her . . . but I could be wrong about you, too!"

Jennifer stood paralyzed as Peer began walking away from her.

Then suddenly, Peer spun around. Even from a distance Jennifer could see he was really angry. "Make up your mind, Jennifer Garrett! I think you're just using Marcia as an excuse not to get involved with me. But, know what? I don't care anymore because I'm out of it as of now!" Then Peer turned and stomped up the dock.

Jennifer turned away. Her eyes filled with tears. She'd made a mess of everything. All she had wanted was for the three of them to be friends. Now, they were mad, all of them. And the person they were maddest at was her!

Chapter Eleven

When Jennifer got back to the cabin, she heard the water running in the bathroom. Marcia was undoubtedly taking a hot shower. The boat ride in her wet clothes, Jennifer knew from experience, must have left Marcia chilled to the bone.

Jennifer glanced into the kitchen. It was nearly one o'clock, and all she'd eaten all day had been a bowl of cereal. Jennifer knew she ought to be hungry, but she just wasn't. In fact, she didn't think she could eat if she tried. Her stomach felt too queasy.

Deciding to lie down, she started up the ladder to the loft. When she saw the torn remains of her journal lying on her bed, it was too much. Throwing herself on top of the mess, Jennifer buried her face in her pillow and began to sob. She felt as if she would cry her heart out.

"Jennifer," a voice startled her. "What's wrong?" Jennifer sat up and peered over the edge of the loft. Marcia stood at the bottom of the ladder in her robe, her hair wrapped in a towel.

"What *isn't* wrong?" Jennifer sniffed.

"Can I come up?" Marcia asked. She sounded truly concerned.

"All right," Jennifer said with a sigh.

Marcia climbed the ladder and sat at the end of Jennifer's bed. "I'm sorry," Marcia said after a long silence. "I tried to be nice today. I really did. I wanted to have fun on the picnic, even after . . ." She let her voice trail off.

"After what?" Jennifer asked, sitting up. She hugged her pillow to her stomach.

"I'm not blind, you know," Marcia said. "I may be dumb, but I'm not blind. I could see the way Peer was looking at you, the way you were looking at him." She handed Jennifer a tissue.

Jennifer took it without meeting Marcia's gaze and wiped her eyes. She wanted to deny what Marcia was saying but she could feel her face color with embarrassment. Her red cheeks, she knew, would give her away.

"You're right," Jennifer said hopelessly. "I never meant for it to happen. I knew that you liked Peer and I decided he was off limits. After all, practically the first thing you did was tell me he was *yours*."

"That's just it," Marcia said sadly. "He wasn't

ever mine. I just didn't want anyone else to have him. It's bad enough that he can't stand me. But to be left out, alone . . ."

"You told me that you liked him and that was enough. If Kate told me she liked a boy at school, I'd never dream of encouraging him to like me no matter how it seemed he felt about Kate."

"But if I was Kate, I wouldn't have made you stay away from a boy you liked and who liked you just because I felt left out. Isn't that true?"

Jennifer wiped away a tear. Then she shrugged. "To tell you the truth, I don't really know. Nothing like this has ever happened to me before. I only know how I felt when I thought you and Peer were a pair, and you were ignoring me."

"How did you feel?" Marcia asked.

Jennifer said, "Terrible! Left out and terrible."

"Then I'm not crazy to feel like that?" Marcia asked.

Jennifer shook her head. "You'd be crazy if you didn't feel like that. That's why Peer and I wanted to include you in our picnic." Jennifer looked at her cousin and sighed. "Sometimes you *act* like a brat," she told Marcia, "but you're not *really* a brat. Inside, I really think you're okay."

"Do you really think so?" Marcia asked hopefully.

Jennifer nodded. "But you're going to have to work at it." Both girls grinned. "Now give me a hand," said Jennifer.

"Doing what?" Marcia asked.

Jennifer picked up a handful of scraps from her journal. "Getting rid of *this*. Let's burn it."

Marcia's cheeks flushed red. "I'm sorry about your journal," she said. "I was jealous that you were telling Kate everything, and me nothing. And then, well, when I read it—it really hurt. I mean, I know most of it was true, but I couldn't face it."

Jennifer looked at the torn-up journal. "I'm sorry too," she said. "I didn't write those things to hurt you. But I had to do something! I was so confused about Peer and the way you were treating me, getting me in trouble with your father and isolating me from everyone. But, what's done is done. Just watch out the next time you see Kate, she'll be furious she didn't get a first hand account of this mess." Jennifer managed a laugh. Marcia smiled too.

"Friends?" she said, offering her hand to Jennifer.

"Friends!" said Jennifer. Impulsively she gave her cousin a hug. "Now let's get rid of this thing."

The girls gathered up the pile of shredded paper and carried it to the fireplace. Jennifer found a match and threw it onto the papers. As the girls watched the journal turn to ashes, Marcia spoke up.

"Jennifer," she said, "there's something I want you to do."

"What," asked Jennifer wistfully.

"Go see Peer, alone." Marcia's sad eyes met Jennifer's. "I know he really likes you. I don't want to keep you two apart—as long as you promise we can still be friends even if you and Peer are together."

Jennifer was silent. She stared into the dying flames of her burning journal.

"Well?" Marcia asked.

"I'm sorry," Jennifer said, "but it's too late."

"But it can't be," Marcia insisted.

Jennifer shook her head. Peer had come right out and said it was too late, hadn't he? Jennifer had no idea what to say to him now. *Oh, hi, Peer! Marcia's just given me her permission to be with you. Let's kiss.* Somehow, she didn't think that would work!

"I'll think about it," Jennifer said evasively.

"Good," said Marcia. "Now how about some cocoa?"

Jennifer laughed shakily. "Are you making it?" she asked.

"Absolutely," replied Marcia. "What are friends for?"

"Peer!" Jennifer called, spotting him ahead of her on the path to the big cabin.

Peer stopped walking and turned around. His dark eyes were set in a fierce scowl which didn't diminish at the sight of her. "Yes, *Jennifer?*" he said.

Suddenly, everything Jennifer had decided to say seemed ridiculous. Maybe Peer hadn't felt all that much for her after all. Maybe the kiss that had seemed so important to her was just an impulse, easily forgotten. Maybe she was just going to annoy him. Her resolve to try to straighten things out with Peer began to wither.

"Well?" he said when she didn't say anything.

"Ummm," Jennifer stammered, trying to think. "Ummm, how about going fishing?"

Peer shook his head. "The fish won't be biting again until this evening. Meanwhile, I've got to clean the fireplace. Mr. Brewster's due back soon, you know."

Jennifer nodded. "Maybe I can help?" she volunteered.

Peer shook his head. "It's a one-man job. But my mother's baking. I'm sure she's got plenty down at our cabin to keep you busy if you've run out of things to do and are feeling bored."

"Sure," Jennifer said. "I'll do that." Jennifer's heart sank as Peer turned away and headed on to the big cabin. He hadn't even said goodbye.

"Oh, Jennifer," Peer called after her. "About fishing . . ."

"Yes?" she said eagerly, turning toward him.

"Talk to my dad. I'm sure *he'd* be glad to take you and your cousin out later on." Peer was colder than she had imagined possible. Jennifer felt like bursting into tears and telling him about everything. But Peer was already on his way into Uncle Ben's cabin. Jennifer's feet felt like lead as she walked to the Finstads' house.

"Hello," Jennifer called through the screen door. The sun behind her made it hard to see into the house. "Anyone here?"

"I'm in the kitchen," Mrs. Finstad called back to her. "Come on in, Jenny."

"Hi," Jennifer said again from the kitchen doorway. "I hear you're baking."

"Hungry?" Mrs. Finstad asked, a merry twinkle in her eye. "Or have you come to help?"

"Oh, I don't know," Jennifer mumbled. The warm kitchen and the sight of a friendly face made Jennifer feel even more like crying.

"Roll up your sleeves, and grab a cookie from the cooling rack on the table. Be careful, they're still hot." Jennifer bit into a cookie. "The bread dough needs kneading, if you feel like helping, and the muffins should come out of the oven in a minute," said Mrs. Finstad.

"How can you do so many different things at one time?" Jennifer asked as she took another oatmeal cookie. "I'd have half of this stuff burned and the other half underdone," she added.

"It takes planning," Mrs. Finstad said. "That, and knowing your recipes inside out. How are the cookies?"

Jennifer nodded, then swallowed. "Delicious," she said, catching a crumb with the back of her hand.

141

"Need some milk to go with that?" Mrs. Finstad asked.

Jennifer shook her head. "I came to help, not to be waited on."

"Who said anything about waiting on you?" Mrs. Finstad demanded, putting her floury hands on her aproned hips. "If you want milk, girl, you'll have to pour it for yourself. The glasses are in the cupboard next to the sink. The milk's in the ice box."

"Thanks," Jennifer said, crossing the kitchen to get herself a glass.

"By the way, where's that cousin of yours?" Mrs. Finstad asked.

Jennifer sighed. "I don't know. Back at our cabin, I guess."

"It's probably none of my business but I'm going to ask anyway. Don't feel you need to answer me if you don't want to," Mrs. Finstad said.

Jennifer took a swallow of milk. Then she said, "What is it?"

"You two girls haven't been getting along too well, have you?" Mrs. Finstad asked.

"If you'd asked me that a few days ago, I would have said you were right. But things are a bit better between us now."

Mrs. Finstad nodded. "Friendships," she said, "take time. I've noticed that Marcia's stopped trailing after Peer. The other times she came here she trailed after Georgie and Karl, Peer's big brothers. I thought it was kind of funny, myself. I even thought Peer might welcome her attention. She's quite a pretty girl—not the little kid that used to trail after his brothers anymore. But he was fit to be tied, madder than a hornet. His dad told him he had to be nice to her, you know, take her fishing.

"It seemed funny to me that you never had any interest in going with them. I thought you were a little stuck up until I got to know you better. You're a darn nice girl, Jenny. The funniest thing of all is that when Marcia started leaving Peer alone, Peer seemed even more upset than ever. I even asked him if he wasn't sorry he was a little short with Marcia, you know, if he wasn't maybe a little sweet on her after all." Mrs. Finstad paused to take another sheet of oatmeal cookies out of the oven. "Well, he just about took my head off then. I had to tell him twice that it was his business entirely and that I was sorry I'd said anything." She looked up from her work to shake her head at Jennifer. "Maybe you can shed a little light on all this."

"What do you mean?" Jennifer asked, her cheeks burning, partly from the heat in the kitchen but mostly from embarrassment.

"You're young," Mrs. Finstad said. "I thought maybe you could explain all this to me. I can't help thinking there's sense to be made of it somewhere but that I'm just too old to see it myself."

"Excuse me," Jennifer said, getting to her feet. "I just remembered something I have to do. Thank you for the milk and cookies." As the screen door banged shut behind her, Jennifer thought she heard Mrs. Finstad cluck her tongue and mutter, "kids!"

"So, that's it in a nutshell," Jennifer concluded, having finished telling Marcia about her encounters with Peer and his mother.

"I suppose Daddy wanted you to come along so I would leave the Finstad boys alone," Marcia mused. "I guess I've made a real fool of myself."

"Not really. I think Mrs. Finstad is kind of fond of you. Anyway, she thinks Peer is moping around because you've stopped asking him to take you fishing. What do you think?" Jennifer asked.

"I think she's wrong and you're nuts. Obviously, Peer is moping around because of you," Marcia said.

"Then why was he so mean to me earlier?" Jennifer demanded.

"He's mad at you—and confused. I suppose he thinks you're playing some sort of game with him. Maybe he even thinks the two of us have been giving him a hard time just to have something to do," Marcia said.

Jennifer looked at her suspiciously. "How do you know all this?"

Marcia looked guilty. "Because I *was* doing that. And maybe Peer thinks we're alike in more ways than just our looks."

"Oh no!" Jennifer gasped, then realized she might be insulting her cousin. "I mean . . ."

"Don't apologize," said Marcia. "I asked for it. The problem is, how do we convince Peer that you're not as obnoxious as your bratty cousin?"

"Marcia—" Jennifer began.

"No," Marcia interrupted. "I'm trying to see things as they are and make some changes— even if that means seeing just how much of a jerk I've been."

"All right," Jennifer agreed. "What's your plan?"

"Well," Marcia began with a sneaky smile, "We'll have to play one little trick on Peer. But I promise he won't mind a bit."

Chapter Twelve

"This isn't another one of Marcia's stunts, is it?" Peer asked suspiciously. "This seems awfully sudden."

Jennifer shrugged, doing her best to look innocent. "That's how colds strike, I guess," Jennifer said. "She probably got a bad chill when she fell in the water. Anyway, Marcia doesn't have anything to take to make her feel better, so I said I'd see if you'd take me to the mainland to get one of those cold remedies."

"I can't believe we don't have something for a cold here," he grumbled irritably. "I have a job tonight that I can't afford to miss out on."

"I did check both cabins," Jennifer assured him. "I even asked your mother if she had anything for a cold, but she said she didn't. Anyway, it isn't even noon yet. A quick trip won't interfere with any plans you have for tonight."

"All right," Peer said grudgingly as he got up from the floor where he'd been sitting to clean the fireplace. "I need to clean up a bit first," he added, dusting off his pants. "I'll meet you at the dock in ten minutes."

Jennifer smiled. "I'll be there!" she cried. Then, realizing how she must sound, Jennifer added in a more serious tone, "Marcia is really uncomfortable with that stuffy nose and fever of hers. I know this is going to mean a lot to her."

"Right," Peer said, wiping his grimy hands on a rag he'd pulled from the back pocket of his jeans.

"Well, then, I'll see you at the dock," Jennifer said, backing out of the room.

So far, so good, Jennifer told herself as she continued to back right out the cabin door. She wanted to dash to her own cabin and tell Marcia that the plan was working so far. But she knew she still had to be careful. Anything might go wrong.

Still, Jennifer felt more confident about their plan being successful than she had on her way to see Peer. He had actually agreed to take her, and Jennifer hadn't expected him to. She thought Peer would tell her to go find his father if she needed a ride somewhere.

Where there's a will, there's a way, Jennifer

147

could almost hear her mother saying. Well, Jennifer had the will, and, thanks to her devious cousin, she had a way, too.

"Dad's letting us take the speed boat," Peer told her when they met on the dock. He'd changed into clean clothes, Jennifer noted. And he had even combed his dark hair to one side. Had he done that for her? she wondered.

Peer dashed her hopes for an easy reconciliation by adding, "That should make the trip faster. I have a lot to do this afternoon, so I'd like to make this as quick as possible." He made it clear that this was just another chore to him, and an unpleasant one at that.

"Okay," Jennifer said, wondering if she shouldn't just call the whole thing off right now. Peer had cared for her once. She'd felt it when they'd kissed, she'd seen it in his eyes. But a person could stop caring—especialy when he thought a girl was playing games with him.

"Come on, then," Peer said, getting into the boat. "Dad fueled her up for us."

Jennifer got in after Peer and sat on the bench seat along the starboard side. That was where she had sat the last time she had been in the speed boat.

"We should both be in the bow," Peer told her. Then before she could get her hopes up that this was some kind of invitation on his part for her to get closer to him, he added, "Otherwise the boat will list to starboard."

"We wouldn't want that," Jennifer mumbled sarcastically as she moved to the front of the boat.

"What?" Peer asked.

"Oh, nothing," she said with a sigh. How, she wondered, was she going to get through to him? If being together wasn't going to be enough, then maybe she should simply try a direct approach. After all, that was what she'd wanted to do in the first place. But she'd let Marcia talk her out of that and into this.

"Peer will laugh at you," Marcia had warned. "And he won't believe you."

But would Peer really laugh? Jennifer looked at him, trying to decide. But then he turned the ignition key, and the motor roared to life. Talking was out of the question, at least for the time being. The direct approach would have to wait.

As they sped through the water, Jennifer had plenty of time to think—and worry. Why had she thought that getting Peer away from his island was the best way to get things back the way they were? Looking at Peer standing up looking over the windshield as he captained the boat, his dark hair flying back in the wind, his strong hands gripping the steering wheel, Jennifer felt a rush of affection. But Jennifer knew that his feelings had been hurt—so hurt, in fact, that he might never speak to her again. She wanted to call it off, but it was too late for that. The ride was nearly over.

"Here we are," Peer shouted as he cut the engine back to a soft purr.

Once they were securely tied to the dock, Peer switched gas tanks, disconnecting the nearly empty tank and hooking up the full one. "Now we're ready to take right off again," he said. His dark eyes held a challenge as he added, "I can run up to the store for the medicine by myself. It would probably be faster that way."

"What's the big rush?" she asked, looking at her watch. "It's only a little after two."

Peer said, "You might not be in a hurry, but I am. Marcia probably is, too."

"I was hoping we could get a soda or something. If we left by three, we'd be home before five," she reasoned. "What time is your job tonight?"

"Nine," Peer replied.

"Nine!" Jennifer exclaimed as they walked briskly down the dock toward town. "What kind of a guiding job starts at nine?"

"I don't suppose you've ever heard of night fishing?" Peer said. Then he answered his own question with, "No, I don't suppose you have."

"But you have tons of time then," Jennifer said, ignoring his sarcastic tone. "I feel I owe you something for agreeing to take this trip. Let me buy you a soda."

They reached the drug store, and Peer opened the door for Jennifer. As she walked past him, he said, "You don't owe me anything. Taking care of you and Marcia is part of my *job.*"

Why, she asked herself as she scanned the shelf of cold remedies, *am I even bothering with this?* Peer seemed to be going out of his way to make the point that there was no longer anything between them.

Picking out a small box of something that promised to do away with cold symptoms for twelve hours, Jennifer gazed in Peer's direction. He was down the aisle from her, examining the different tubes of lip balm. Suddenly, Jennifer could almost feel again the brief kiss they'd shared, and she knew that Peer *was* worth the bother. If only she could get through to him.

So far the trip to the mainland hadn't followed the scenario she'd dreamed up with Marcia. Jennifer hadn't carried on the small talk with Peer during the boat ride like she was supposed to. And when Jennifer offered to buy him a soda, Peer was supposed to have insisted on making it lunch instead of just a soda. Over lunch, they would stare into each other's eyes. Then, heading back to the boat, arm in arm, they would pause and kiss. By the time they got back to the island . . .

Jennifer sighed. *Are dreams always better than reality?* she asked herself as she made her way to the cash register.

"Is that all you're going to get?" Peer asked, suddenly appearing at her side.

"I thought so. What else do you think I should get? I mean, this does say it works on all major symptoms," Jennifer told him.

Peer stared at her intently for a moment. "I guess we should get going then," he said, whisking her out the door with her bag in hand.

"How about that soda?" she asked. "It could just be a quick one."

Peer shook his head. "Dad has things for me to do. I need to get back."

"I understand," Jennifer said. But she couldn't stop herself from sighing.

"Well . . ." Peer said, glancing at her out of the corner of his eye. He slowed down a little bit. "Maybe just a quick one—if it's that important to you."

"Oh, no. I don't want to keep you," she insisted.

"Dad won't mind. Come on," he said with increasing conviction. "It'll be my treat!"

Jennifer had to take two steps for his every one as she hustled to keep up with him. In a matter of seconds, they were at the ice cream parlor next to the hardware store.

"This place is only open in the summer," Peer said, holding the screen door for her. "They have great ice cream. What do you want?"

"I'll just have a Coke," she told him, wondering to what she should attribute Peer's sudden change in attitude.

"Oh, come on," he coaxed her, "have a hot fudge sundae. I'm going to."

"I'll just have a bite of yours," she said.

"No, you won't. You'll either have your own or you won't have any." Then turning to the boy behind the counter, Peer said, "We'll have two hot fudge sundaes—with peppermint ice cream?" He looked over at Jennifer, and she nodded with a grin.

When they sat down to eat, Peer dug into his sundae with gusto. Jennifer was speechless at his sudden cheerfulness.

"Don't you like it?" Peer asked when he'd finished and Jennifer hadn't.

"It's delicious," she assured him, "but it's too much for me. Do you want to finish mine?"

Peer grinned from ear to ear. "If you're sure you don't want it!" He looked just like a little boy as he pulled Jennifer's nearly full dish in front of himself.

"Okay," he said when he'd finished, "let's go!" Briskly, he led the way to the dock.

When they got to the boat, it dawned on Jennifer that their time together was nearly over. So far they weren't any closer than they'd been before. Peer did seem less hostile, but he was hardly falling over himself making declarations of love to her the way she'd hoped.

She untied the boat and hopped aboard.

Peer already had the motor running, and put the engine in gear. As soon as they were in open water, Peer pulled the throttle into high gear. Then, without another word, they were off, speeding back to the island.

They hadn't gone far when the engine began to sputter. Jennifer watched Peer fiddle with the choke. But that didn't seem to help. The sputtering just got worse.

"Is something wrong with the engine?" Jennifer asked.

"It does seem that way," Peer said. He looked up from the steering wheel and scanned the horizon. "We'd better just land somewhere so I can check this out." All at once, he started laughing.

"What's so funny?" Jennifer demanded.

"Doesn't that island over there look familiar to you?" Peer asked, pointing at the small island in front of them.

Jennifer could scarcely believe her eyes! It was the same island they'd landed on during the storm and the same island they'd tried to picnic on so disastrously. *Talk about bad luck!* Jennifer thought.

"It can't be!" she cried.

"I can't believe it either," Peer said. "But it's the same island, all right. Maybe we've just gotten a little water or sand in the gas line. That's easily remedied. Anyway, I doubt if it's anything to get too upset about."

"What about your job tonight?" she asked, amazed that he seemed so unconcerned about this sudden turn of events. Jennifer seemed to be more concerned than Peer.

"I'm sure I can fix whatever's wrong," Peer said. "I've been working on boat motors for years, you know."

"What can I do?" Jennifer asked. "There must be some way I can help."

Peer shrugged. "I don't know. I guess you could do a little fishing if you wanted to. That way, if we do get stranded overnight or something, we'll have something for our dinner." He grinned at her.

"Do you really think we could get stranded overnight?" Jennifer asked, beginning to worry despite herself.

Peer shook his head. "No. Probably not. Anyway, it would be no big deal if we were. This boat has a lot of stuff in it, you know, like blankets, a tarp, tools, matches, just about everything we could want, including two spinning rods and a well-equipped tackle box." As Peer finished, the motor gave one last, feeble sputter, then was silent.

Luckily, they were close enough to shore to drift the rest of the way. When they were finally close enough, Jennifer, already on the bow of the boat, jumped ashore. Once she'd secured the boat, Peer joined her.

"Well," he said, after clearing his throat, "where would you like to fish?"

Jennifer shrugged. "Are you sure I can't do something more useful than fish?"

"Can you take an engine apart and put it back together?" he asked. Jennifer shook her head. "Then go fish. I can take care of the motor."

"I could hand you tools or something," Jennifer offered. Now that they were alone on a deserted island, she didn't want to go off by herself.

But Peer was insistent. "Take this rod and go on. There's a sand bar on the western edge of this island where the fishing is pretty good."

Reluctantly, Jennifer accepted the rod and started up the rocks. She was just a few steps from Peer when she slipped on a jagged rock and fell hard.

"Oh!" she cried, trying to get up. Peer rushed to her.

"Jenny!" he said, "what's wrong?"

"I feel so dumb," she told him. "I think I've broken the rod."

"Don't worry about that. Are you hurt?" he asked. He wrapped his hand around hers, and she felt a powerful current run between them. Gently, Peer began stroking her hand.

"I don't know," she said. "I think I might have twisted my ankle."

"Do you think you can stand on it?" he asked.

Jennifer made a move to get up but quickly sat back down, grabbing her left ankle with both hands as she did. "Oh," she moaned, "it hurts."

"Here," Peer told her, brushing aside her hands so he could touch the ankle, "let me have a look." He moved Jennifer's ankle slightly and said, "Does this hurt?"

"Yes!" she cried. "Please, don't!"

Peer shook his head. "I feel so dumb."

"It's not your fault." Jennifer sniffed slightly. "I'm the one who's sorry," she told him. "I should have been more careful. I must have tripped on something."

"But it is my fault," Peer insisted, sitting down next to her. "We don't even have to be here."

"What do you mean?" Jennifer asked. "How could we have helped it? The motor . . ."

"The motor is fine," he admitted sheepishly.

"You mean there's nothing wrong with the boat?" Jennifer exclaimed.

157

Peer shook his head. "We just ran out of gas, that's all. I didn't really switch to the full gas tank when we got to the mainland. As soon as I hook up the second tank, we can take off."

"You mean you deliberately stranded us here?" she asked, amazed. Jennifer suddenly felt like singing, despite the pain in her ankle. *He does like me!*

"I just wanted to be alone with you. I wasn't sure if you'd agree to stopping if I came right out and asked you—I haven't been very pleasant lately. I know it was dumb. You've got every right to be mad."

Jennifer took his hand in hers. "So do you," she said, smiling. "We didn't really have to go to the mainland at all."

"You mean there was some cold stuff back on the island?" he asked.

Jennifer shook her head and said, "No. There really isn't any cold stuff on the island. But Marcia doesn't really have a cold."

Peer looked at Jennifer, and Jennifer held his gaze. All at once, they both started laughing.

Finally, Peer said, "The only question now is whether to take you back to the mainland for an X ray or back to the island."

"Oh, Peer," Jennifer whimpered, looking down at her ankle which had begun to swell. "I've gone and ruined everything!" Her eyes filled with tears.

"No," he assured her, smoothing a wisp of dark hair from her forehead. "You haven't ruined anything." He leaned still closer and gently traced her lips with his finger. "Don't worry, Jenny. Everything will be all right." Then, before she even realized what was happening, he was kissing her.

"Oh, Peer," Jennifer murmured once their kiss had ended. "I'm so glad we finally got this sorted out." She put her arms around his neck and kissed him again.

"Jenny," he said, shaking his head as he gazed into her eyes. "I've been so dumb."

"We've both been dumb," she corrected him softly.

Peer stood up and looked down at the boat. "I'll go change the tanks. Then I'll come back for you. Since we're more than halfway to the mainland, I guess we should go there first, you know, just to make sure nothing is broken."

Jennifer watched him slide down the rocks to the boat, and she knew she was in love.

Chapter Thirteen

"Come with us," Jennifer insisted. "All we're going to do is fish. It'll be fun."

"You're going out on a balmy, moonlit night, and you're *actually* going to fish?" Marcia cried. "I think those doctors must have X-rayed the wrong part of you. It's your brain you sprained, not your ankle. We've only got a few days left, and I think you two ought to spend some more time alone."

"We were alone the other night when we went to the movies over on the mainland. Besides, what'll you do if you don't come with us?" Jennifer asked.

Marcia held up the paperback she'd set down on the couch when Jennifer had first interrupted her. "I'm kind of into this," she said.

Jennifer examined the cover curiously. "Is it any good?"

"Are you kidding?" Marcia said. "If it was any better, it would probably be outlawed."

Jennifer giggled. "Well, if you're sure you don't want to go . . ."

"I'm sure. And quit looking at me like I'm being noble. You two deserve a little time on your own. And anyway, fishing is still not my idea of an exciting time."

Jennifer laughed. She might look a little bit like her cousin Marcia, but Marcia and Jennifer were nothing alike on the inside. Marcia would only go fishing if something besides catching fish was her ultimate goal. Jennifer, on the other hand, really did love to fish. There was both an excitement and a peacefulness to fishing—not to mention the great eating that followed success—that Jennifer enjoyed.

"All right," Jennifer said, secretly pleased for a chance to be alone with Peer. "I give up. I'll see you later. We shouldn't be too late."

"Have fun," Marcia called after her.

The moon was full, lighting up the night, bathing everything in its creamy, yellow glow. Jennifer wanted to skip down to the dock where she could already see Peer's dark silhouette against the shimmering water. But her ankle, though better, was still weak. She didn't want to risk hurting it again. The couple of days she'd had to spend off her feet while she waited for the swelling to go down had been two days too many for her.

"Finally!" Peer called when Jennifer reached the dock. "Did you talk Marcia into joining us?"

"I tried," Jennifer told him, "but I failed."

"Good," Peer said, getting to his feet.

"Peer!" Jennifer admonished him. "I thought you agreed that it would be nice if Marcia came with us."

"I did, but is there anything wrong with wanting to be alone with the girl I'm crazy about?" he asked, stepping closer to her.

"No," she said as he put his arms around her.

Burying his face in her hair, Peer hugged her tighter. Then he gently tilted her face toward his. "Oh, no you don't," she said, slipping out of his embrace before he could kiss her.

"What's wrong?" he asked softly.

"I just want to kiss you first," she said playfully, wrapping her arms around his neck.

"Hmmm," Peer murmured a few moments later. "I respect a lady who knows what she wants."

"Well, okay, since I'm the boss . . . Come on, now, into the boat," Jennifer said, giving him a playful push. "I didn't cruise around with you all afternoon marking good fishing spots with the buoys just to end up spending the evening on the dock kissing you."

"Now I see where I stand with you—second fiddle to a fish. Into the boat then, Miss Garrett," Peer said, executing a sweeping bow. Jennifer climbed carefully in while Peer remained on the dock.

"Hey," she cried delightedly, looking around the boat, "you've been busy, haven't you?" Peer had lashed a flashlight to the long handle of the fish net. A larger, battery powered lantern was fastened to the boat's windshield. Jennifer noticed still another lantern on the red leather driver's seat.

"We've got to have light. Even with the moon helping out the way it is, we've got to be seen by other boats," Peer explained as he untied the boat.

"I'm so excited!" Jennifer said. "Let's not waste another minute."

Peer hopped into the boat, shoving them away from the dock as he did. He started up the engine and they were off. Peer kept the boat at a moderately low speed as they sliced through the trail the full moon was making on the black lake water.

Peer easily located the first of their markers. "It's really shallow here, so we'll have to be careful," he warned Jennifer. "I think I'll drive the boat and let you fish. Remember that first big walleye you landed?" he asked.

Jennifer nodded. "I'll never forget that!" She

remembered the thrill of Peer's arms around her the day she caught her first fish.

Peer smiled at her tenderly. "I won't either. Hey, whatever happened to that fish, anyway? It just sort of disappeared."

Jennifer laughed. "No, it didn't. I let it go. I'm glad I did, too." With that she pushed the button on the reel and felt the line release, dropping the lure into the water with a plunk.

"Okay," Peer said, "now you have to concentrate. It's really shallow here and you don't want to get your line hung up."

Jennifer nodded, but, before she could say that she *always* concentrated, she felt a strike. "I've got something!" she exclaimed.

"Easy now," Peer urged. "Don't get too excited. Remember, you've got to get that hook set or your fish will get away."

"I'm sure it's already set," Jennifer said. "I've never *felt* a fish hit the hook that hard before!"

"Hang on," Peer told her. "I'll anchor the boat and help you bring it in."

Jennifer felt the fish fighting. As soon as it stopped, she began reeling in. But then it began to fight again.

"I'm right beside you," Peer said. "I've got the net. All you have to do is get the fish to the boat."

"It's huge!" Jennifer said.

"Don't let your line go slack," Peer warned, "or

it'll get away so fast you won't even know what happened until it's too late."

The line started screeching again as the fish pulled it back out of Jennifer's reel. "It's a fighter!" she told Peer.

Peer laughed. "I'm afraid it's met its match this time. You're a fighter, too, Jenny." With that, Peer flicked on the flashlight that was fastened to the fish net. "I see it!" he cried. "It's a beauty! Just a little more, Jenny, and I'll be able to net him."

Once they had the fish netted, Jennifer saw that he was the same size as the first fish she'd caught on the trip. "Do you think this could be the same fish?" she asked Peer.

Peer shrugged. "It would be a real long-shot, but I guess it's possible." He carefully worked the hook out of the fish's mouth. "Anything's possible," he added, smiling at her again. Then he said, "Hand me the stringer."

"Let's let him go," Jennifer said.

"Let him go! Again? This is a trophy fish. You could have him mounted and hang him in your room back home," Peer told her.

Jennifer giggled. "Wouldn't my mother love that? No, I want to let him go. Like you told me, the littler fish are better eating anyway. This guy's lived around here a long time. I know how I feel about leaving this beautiful place. It's just not fair."

"Are you talking about this fish, or are you talking about yourself?" Peer asked.

"Give him to me," Jennifer ordered. Peer handed her the fish, and Jennifer threw it back. She heard him hit the water, but it was too dark to see him swim away. "Goodbye," she whispered, suddenly sad. Then she turned to Peer. "That's what you're going to have to do to me, you know."

"Throw you back?" he asked. Jennifer nodded, and Peer took her in his arms. Then he laughed, kissing the top of her head.

"I meant what I said, you know. I'll be leaving in just a few days. We might never see each other again."

"Of course we'll see each other again," Peer assured her. His voice sounded strong and very definite. "You'll be back—maybe next summer, maybe sooner. But you'll be back all right." Then his lips found hers, and Jennifer knew Peer was right. She'd be back to this island, back to him, again and again . . . if only in her dreams.

We hope you enjoyed reading this book. If you would like to receive further information about titles available in the Bantam series, just write to the address below, with your name and address: Kim Prior, Bantam Books, 61–63 Uxbridge Road, Ealing, London W5 5SA

If you live in Australia or New Zealand and would like more information about the series, please write to:

Sally Porter
Transworld Publishers
(Australia) Pty Ltd
15–23 Helles Avenue
Moorebank
NSW 2170
AUSTRALIA

Kiri Martin
Transworld Publishers (NZ) Ltd
Cnr. Moselle and Waipareira Avenues
Henderson
Auckland
NEW ZEALAND

All Bantam Young Adult books are available at your bookshop or newsagent, or can be ordered from the following address: Corgi/Bantam Books, Cash Sales Department, PO Box 11, Falmouth, Cornwall, TR10 9EN.

Please list the title(s) you would like, and send together with a cheque or postal order. You should allow for the cost of book(s) plus postage and packing charges as follows: 80p for the first book, 20p for each additional book ordered up to a maximum charge of £2.00.

Please note that payment must be made in pounds sterling; other currencies are unacceptable.

(The above applies to readers in the UK and Republic of Ireland only)

BFPO customers, please allow for the cost of the book(s) plus the following for postage and packing: 80p for the first book and 20p for each additional book.

Overseas customers, please allow £1.50 for postage and packing for the first book, £1.00 for the second book, and 30p for each subsequent title ordered.

It's hot! It's sexy! It's fun!

Baby's life changes forever when she meets Johnny. For he is an electrifying dancer, and he shows Baby what dancing is *really* all about – the heat, the rhythm and the excitement . . .

A sensational series based on the characters from the top-grossing *Dirty Dancing* movie and television series.

1. BABY, IT'S YOU
2. HELLO, STRANGER
3. SAVE THE LAST DANCE FOR ME
4. BREAKING UP IS HARD TO DO
5. STAND BY ME
6. OUR DAY WILL COME

Created by Francine Pascal

Caitlin is Francine Pascal's most dazzling and irresistible
heroine. Follow her story, from high school
days to womanhood.

CAITLIN: THE LOVE TRILOGY

Written by Joanne Campbell

1. LOVING
2. LOVE LOST
3. TRUE LOVE

CAITLIN: THE PROMISE TRILOGY COLLECTION

Written by Diana Gregory

TENDER PROMISES, PROMISES BROKEN and A
NEW PROMISE: in one three-book top-value collection.

CAITLIN: THE FOREVER TRILOGY

Written by Diana Gregory

1. DREAMS OF FOREVER
2. FOREVER AND ALWAYS
3. TOGETHER FOREVER

First Kiss

First love . . . first kiss!

A terrific new series that focuses firmly on that most important moment in any girl's life – falling in love for the very first time ever.

Available soon from wherever Bantam paperbacks are sold!

1. Head Over Heels by Susan Blake
2. Love Song by Suzanne Weyn
3. Falling for You by Carla Bracale
4. The Perfect Couple by Helen Santori